THE MERCI TRAIN
WEDDING DRESS

BY

LINDA BATEN JOHNSON

Chapter 1

1949

Betty Jackson's knock on the door's frame received a gruff "This better be good!" from the slump-shouldered man who didn't look at her.

She sucked in a deep breath, then stepped inside the editor's inner sanctum. "Mr. Roark, it's Betty Jackson. I left your mail on the secretary's desk. Do you have a story for me to cover today?"

"You!" Roark leaned back in his chair and laced his fingers behind his head. "Back again? Betty, I admire your doggedness, but you have three strikes against you. You're female, your skin's the wrong color, and you're too young. And only one of those conditions is ever going to change."

Today, she detected a hint of admiration for her persistence. "Don't want to change, just want to be a reporter for the Parrish Gazette, the best newspaper in Louisiana and with the best editor in the business."

"How long have you been beating on my door?" Roark moved his hands from behind his head to rest on his paunchy belly.

"This is my thirty-seventh day, Sir."

1

"And every day, I've told you the same thing. Maybe I made a mistake hiring you for the delivery job. Anyway, I've already got a gal for the social beat."

"I don't want the social scene, Sir. I want news." Betty lifted her chin, hoping she looked confident, despite the turmoil she felt in her stomach.

Roark pointed to the chair in front of his desk. "Can you write?"

He'd never invited her to sit, so she eased into the chair, perching on the front edge. "I can write."

"Oh?" He leaned forward. "And where did you get your training?"

"You trained me, Sir. I've been reading your newspaper since I was a kid. I rewrite five stories a day, telling them in a different way. I do one front page, one social, one sports, one human interest, and one obit. Would you like to see some of them?" She rummaged through the bag she'd positioned next to the chair.

"No." He tapped his red pencil on the desk. "Always liked the pesky type. You eighteen yet?"

She nodded.

"Can't promise I'll ever give you a byline. You know the prejudice in this burg." He swiveled in his chair.

She kept her mouth shut, a practice she'd learned as a child. It was best to keep quiet when adults considered decisions.

"You can't work in the bullpen either. Fellows wouldn't like it. The other girl drops her copy off. That okay with you?"

She nodded again, picturing the other "girl" writing for the Gazette, a severe-looking spinster who did the social news.

"Pay's based on inch of print, not on how much you write, and I'm known for slashing copy, making it bleed." He tapped the paper on his desk which was riddled with red marks.

"That's why I want to work for you."

He ignored her comment and checked off items on the tablet by his right hand. "I'll give you one story—only one and no more. You can say you've written for the Gazette and stay out of my hair."

"Thank you." She wanted to jump out of the chair, but forced herself to remain calm.

Mr. Roark rubbed his bald head. "Guess that was a bad analogy about staying out of my hair. But seriously, young'un, stay out of my office. Here's your chance for a story. The Merci Train car is coming to New Orleans tomorrow. Merci means thanks in French, and the citizens of France are giving each state a boxcar full of gifts as a thank-you for the food we sent them in 1947. Know anything about it?"

"Not yet, but I will."

"Now, let me get back to work. It's one story, and that's all. You got it? Don't want to start something, have every Tom, Dick, or Harrietta hanging around my door begging for stories."

She bobbed her head. "One story. Thank you."

"Now get out and don't come back."

"I'll bring you a great story you'll want to run on page one." Her cheeks ached from her broad smile.

"Be content with two inches on the back page—if your work is good enough. I don't like to do rewrites." He waved her out of the office with the back of his hand.

She wanted to throw up her hands and dance, but asked in a controlled voice. "Should I bring my story directly to you?"

"No. Leave your masterpiece at the front desk. And Betty, write in an upside-down triangle with the who, what, when, where, why, and how in the first paragraph. That might be all you get to see in print. I should be able to cut from the bottom to top on reporting."

"Triangle. Thank you, thank you, Mr. Roark."

"And nothing flowery. Close the door on your way out."

When she turned to say thank you a third time, he was filling another sheet of paper with red marks.

Merci Train? New Orleans? She should start at the local depot.

The train's rail beds served as the color demarcation line in her hometown of Jolson with the whites ensconced on the north side of the railroad tracks. Separate stores, separate schools, separate churches, but that was changing, thanks to the sacrifice of boys whose skin was the same color as hers. Her brother served with volunteers from the town in his military regiment, and when the mayor called the names of soldiers who perished, he included Billy. When she passed the memorial column in the center of town, she always traced the letters of her brother's name, William Jackson, chiseled in the marble.

Betty fashioned questions in her mind for the people at the depot. Maybe she'd stop by the library first. The knot in her stomach returned. She didn't want to mess up her big opportunity. Who? What? When? Where? Why? How? She'd knock on the library's big oak doors and hope that Mrs. Warren would come out to see her. She should be the first to know about her success.

The name of the librarian's husband was also carved on the column in the center of the town square. To honor him and all soldiers, Helen Warren, only a handful of years older than Betty, championed a library open-door policy. The city fathers vetoed the idea. Instead, they gave Mrs. Warren the right to run a bookmobile for the people on the other side of the tracks. Betty's family took advantage of the myriad of books, and she shepherded her siblings to Mrs. Warren's story time where the librarian made books come alive outside the library on wheels. Helen Warren fostered Betty's desire to become a reporter, and helped her plan her strategy to gain access to Mr. Roark's newspaper staff by wrangling her a job as a mail delivery girl.

Helen opened the library door and lifted her eyebrows. "I can tell you have good news."

Betty wrinkled her nose and clapped her hands—quietly. "He gave me a story. Finally. You said he would. I'd have stopped going to his office each day if it hadn't been for you."

5

"Noah Roark is a good man, just needs some prodding. What's the story? Tell me everything." Helen led her to the bench in front of the library.

Mrs. Warren, who insisted Betty call her "Helen," could place books on the top shelf without a footstool, but she always wore pumps when she worked. Her russet hair fell to her shoulders with just the right amount of curl, and her green eyes sparkled with affection as she parceled out books to readers or counseled Betty on how to achieve her personal dreams. Today she wore a dove-colored skirt with a soft pink blouse, closed at the throat with a broach of hand-painted white roses. Her seams were perfectly straight. Her attire said she was a professional, a lady, what Betty aspired to be.

Betty relished the retelling and her friend's excitement. She finished with a request for help. "Now, I've got to find out everything there is to know about this Merci Train that's coming to New Orleans."

"I should make a trip to New Orleans. We can go together. I'll enjoy watching you chase down your first story." Helen's lips parted in a half smile. "Betty, I want you to succeed, but…"

"I know. Reporting is a man's job."

Helen patted her hand. "In Louisiana, it's a white man's arena. Promise me you'll be careful."

Betty crisscrossed her heart with her finger. "Cross my heart and hope to die."

Chapter 2

Sam Parker knew the Dean's Office well. He'd earned top marks at Southern University in Scotlandville, Louisiana, since he'd returned from the war. Using the GI bill, he managed to attend classes, study, and work two jobs to help out his family and keep his head above water.

"I've got another honor for you." Dean Keaton pumped Sam's hand and ushered him toward an overstuffed green leather chair.

"Honor?" Sam allowed himself to relax against the back of the chair. "You might have the wrong person."

"No, you're the right person." The dean rubbed his hands together. "Received a call from the Merci Train Committee. They want a member of the 761st to serve as part of the welcome guard when the train arrives."

Sam tilted his head. "Merci Train?"

"The Train of Gratitude, known as the Merci Train, contains carloads of gifts from French people to American citizens as thanks for the Friendship Train of 1947. Do you remember when Americans collected food in 1947 to send to the starving Europeans?"

"I do. My sisters donated evaporated milk for the train at the local theater, and the manager allowed them to watch a Saturday morning double feature for free."

"Well, the French sent forty-nine train cars loaded with gifts to the United States. Each state receives a car. The forty-ninth one is for Washington, D.C. and Hawaii to share."

"The French people were kind to us, treated us with respect." Sam often mused about the time he'd been on leave in France. "People over there didn't seem to notice the color of my skin. I've often wondered if their actions had been post-war giddiness or their everyday perspective."

"Well someone in France felt kindness about a person named Sam Parker." The dean continued, "Newspapers say there's a gift on the car earmarked for a man with your name."

"Just got the chills, maybe someone walking over my grave." Sam shivered. "My name's pretty common."

"Back to the honor guard duty assignment. Louisiana welcomes her car in New Orleans on Sunday, February 13, with a parade down Canal Street." The dean eyed him from head to toe. "Can you still get into your uniform after two years of eating Mama's home cooking?"

"The buttons do strain a bit, but I'd like to participate. When and where do I report?"

* * *

Sam held up his thumb by the side of the road on Saturday afternoon. He'd allotted extra travel time since he had to hitch the eighty miles from Baton Rouge to New Orleans. His daddy's brother lived in New Orleans, so he'd have a place to spend the night when he arrived. Good Fortune smiled on his travels, and his feet were under Uncle Charlie's table before the moon rose.

Female cousins warned him to watch out for wanton women as he dressed in his uniform the next morning. They brushed his shoulders free of lint and dust, admired his gleaming shoes, and teased him about the freckles that still danced across his nose and cheeks.

"You're sure handsome." The oldest of the four young ladies announced. "My best friend is hunting for a nice, good-looking guy to take home to meet her daddy."

Uncle Charlie shushed the girls. "Leave the man alone. He's not in the marriage market. Sam has big dreams, going to make us all proud one day, aren't you, Sam?"

"I'll do my best, Sir." The burden of his family's and extended family's expectations wearied him.

***

With the Merci Car mounted on a flat-bed trailer pulled by a large truck, the parade meandered down Canal Street. The forty-nine railroad cars sent to America filled with gifts were the French "forty and eights," used in World War I to transport forty men or eight horses. However the gauge of the French tracks were a different size than America's railroad tracks, so the gifts in the beautifully painted cars had to be shipped on platforms to the different states. Preceded by marching bands, clowns on tricycles, jugglers, and dance teams, Sam marched with other soldiers beside the forty and eight gift car decorated with medallions representing French provinces. The other soldiers hadn't objected to his presence, a tribute to his light skin color.

Crowds roared approval and threw beads and doubloons toward the train car, a Mardi Gras reverse. When they stopped near the scaffolding erected for the official podium, the guard halted. They stood at attention while the city officials droned on about Louisiana's achievements, New Orleans hospitality, and lengthy introductions of everyone on the platform. During the speech, Sam received sharp jabs from the soldier on his right.

"Just noticed your insignia, the 761st. That's the Louisiana black group. You trying to pass for white?"

"No."

The man poked him again. "Your kind shouldn't serve in an honor guard."

The soldier on Sam's left craned his neck toward the speaker. "Leave him alone, Burton. He fought just like we did." He nodded slightly to Sam. "My name's Sanford Dickens. My rude friend is Burton Loughman." Dickens rolled his eyes and nodded to the platform. "Politicians sure can talk. Looks like the mayor is finally finishing."

The mayor yielded the podium to the Merci Train Committee Chairwoman, who rivaled the mayor's effusiveness. Helpers opened the sliding car doors to show the crates packed inside. "We will carefully catalog the contents of each box, but Louisiana has something special in its car, a gift from a French medical doctor to one of our Louisiana soldiers, Sam Parker. The letter says the gift is in crate seven. Should I read you the letter? Should we open the crate?"

The audience roared approval and she exaggerated opening of the envelope. She shook out the thin paper and adjusted her glasses.

"Honorable Louisiana friends, I send a personal gift to Sam Parker, a soldier who came ashore at Omaha Beach." She paused and placed her hand over her heart before continuing. "The young man helped save the life of an injured French resistance fighter, one of those who met the Americans during the bloody battle that day. Mr. Parker carried the Frenchman to the field hospital where a medic saved the man's life by amputating his left arm. That young man was my son, and I want Sam Parker, of the 761st Tank Battalion, and a native of Scotlandville..." The woman's voice trailed off as murmurs and boos erupted from the crowd when the audience realized the heroic subject of the letter was a man of color.

The mayor edged the woman away from the microphone. "That gift should be presented in a private ceremony. The hour is getting late, and you've all been very patient. This efficient lady has a group of helpers who will record each item as the crates are opened." He turned to the lady. "When will that happen?"

The lady held up two fingers.

11

The mayor nodded. "She'll start the proceedings in two weeks. I'm sure we'll have a list of all the gifts published in the newspaper. Now, let's have a little music to end the festivities."

The guard was dismissed, and Sam tried to retreat, but Burton grabbed the front of his uniform. "Name on your uniform is Parker, and you're in the 761st. You think you're some sort of hero."

"No, Sir. I'm just a soldier." Sam backed up.

"Lay off, Burton. He never did anything to you." Sanford Dickens moved next to Sam. "Was that you described in the letter?"

Sam shrugged. "I'm not sure."

Burton stood directly in front of Sam. "Why were you even in this parade?"

The peacemaker ignored his friend's comment and addressed Sam. "After Omaha Beach, the 761st was with Patton, right? And in the Battle of the Bulge."

"We were, Sir." Sam grinned. "General Patton requested us. He said we were the first Negro tankers to ever fight in the American Army and that he wouldn't have asked for us if we weren't good."

Burton waved his arms, ending with a mock salute. "Can't be much of a hero if you're still alive."

Sanford grabbed Burton's arm. "Burton, you've been drinking. Don't know how you managed to march, but one more won't hurt you. Let's go celebrate the Merci Car's arrival in Louisiana."

Burton jerked away. "Thought you might want to go share a beer with your new buddy. He won't be so pretty after I rearrange his arrogant face."

Burton reached for Sam, brandishing a knife pulled from his pocket.

Sanford stepped between Sam and Burton, just as the blade slashed.

Sanford clutched his throat.

Sam fell to his knees, instinctively placing his hand over the wound spurting blood.

"No! Sanford, why did you jump in front of him?" Burton stared wide-eyed at the two men on the ground. "You ignorant fool, what are you doing? Get your filthy hands off my friend," Burton yelled.

People circled them, closing in, but Sam concentrated on the man whose blood stained his hands.

"I told you to get away from him!" Burton tugged at Sam's hands.

"I need to stop the flow." Sam maintained pressure on Sanford's wound and spoke slowly to Burton. "Sir, white medics on the battlefield told me that when blood spurts from wounds, you must keep pressure on the spot. Your friend needs immediate help. Perhaps you should call a doctor."

"Get away from him." When Burton chopped Sam's hand away from Sanford's neck, blood gushed out, hitting him in the face." Burton turned and puked. He wiped his mouth with the back of his hands and staggered out of the ring of observers, yelling as he left. "I'll get help, but you better not let him die, you uppity fool."

13

Sam continued firm pressure on Sanford's neck. "You'll be all right, Sir. Help is on the way."

Had this nice, gentle man survived the battlefields of Europe only to be killed in his home state?

Sirens screamed and Burton waved the ambulance to the place where Sam knelt over ashen-faced Sanford.

A man with a black bag barked commands, and a stretcher appeared. "Man's pal said he was spurting blood."

"Yes, Sir. Neck wound, Sir. Kept pressure on it, but his color is bad, and his hands are turning cold." Sam kept his gaze down.

"Then we better get him to an operating room. Don't move your hand. You'll have to come in the ambulance with us." He turned to the medical team. "Get him on the stretcher."

Sam grimaced, knowing he would not be welcome in the white hospital, even if he was saving a man's life.

"You a medic in the war?" The doctor placed blankets over the man on the stretcher, working around Sam's hands.

"No, Sir. But the doctor for our unit often requested my help. He said that I was the rare one who could handle the blood, the yelling, and the terror."

"Maybe you could be useful in our hospital. We're always looking for orderlies. Want me to put in a word for you?" The doctor raised his eyebrows in question.

"Not right now, Sir. I'm going to Southern on the GI bill, hope to get a chance to go to medical school." Sam didn't look up.

14

The doctor laughed. "You know of any medical schools who would take you?"

Sam shrugged his shoulders. "There's a couple. Meharry, in Tennessee, takes men of color."

"That right?" The doctor stumbled as the ambulance screeched to a stop. "Guess the world's changing."

The doors flew open, and again, the doctor issued commands. "Nurse, when I count to three, put your hand on the wound and keep it firm until we get him into the operating room. Got it?"

"Yes, Sir." The nurse waited by Sam as they listened for the doctor's short countdown.

The medical group pushed through the doors of the hospital, leaving Sam in the parking lot, hands red with blood.

* * *

A red Ford Super Deluxe stopped, and a white woman rolled down the passenger-side window. "Need a ride, Soldier?"

Could his day get any worse? He touched the brim of his hat. "No thank you, Ma'am. I'll be walking."

Then the most beautiful woman he'd ever seen jumped out of the rear seat and raced around the car. "We saw what you did. You were very brave."

Her voice was as warm and melodious as a warbling mockingbird. He judged her slender frame to be about the height of his oldest sister, who stood five foot two. He stared open-mouthed. What was she doing in a car with white folks? Her skin was an exquisite cinnamon shade. And those dark chocolate eyes sat above a little button nose that called out to be kissed.

"You were courageous. It's okay if you go with us." She indicated the other woman. "Mrs. Warren is the librarian in Jolson, a neighborhood near Baton Rouge. She and her friend, Mr. Claude Roark, came to New Orleans to see the Merci Train, and they invited me to come with them."

"Invited you?" He heard the shock and surprise in his voice.

Claude Roark, now out of the Ford, unlocked the trunk and handed him two towels. "Always carry towels. You can clean your hands. My daddy's the editor of the local newspaper. He strongly suggested I take Helen and this one to New Orleans. Now, where are you headed?"

"I go to Southern University in Scotlandville, that's north of Baton Rouge." His feet were rooted to the ground. "But I can thumb it home."

The woman with the reddish-colored hair got out and opened the back seat door for him. "We insist. You must come with us. We're going to the same place, you two get in the back. Betty Jackson helps me with the bookmobile, but today she is a reporter, and you might be her story."

Betty Jackson. The beauty had a name, but not the name he would have given her. She should be called Jewel or Star, or Diamond, because everything about her sparkled. Her eyes, her mouth, her turned-up nose, her bouncy walk, her slim figure.

16

Claude Roark's voice sounded urgent. "Get in, and both of you should keep your heads down. There's a policeman headed this way."

Sam obeyed, hoping his acceptance of this ride wouldn't be a mistake.

Chapter 3

Betty scooted next to Sam in the back seat, while Claude edged the Ford into traffic.

"Maybe they'll only notice me, and not you two." Helen checked on them framed in her vanity mirror.

"I appreciate the ride, but I'm happy to hitchhike. That's how I got to New Orleans." Sam's comment went unacknowledged.

"We'll soon be out of the city." The man shifted gears.

"Helen's friend is a good driver. He's the son of the local newspaper editor, the one who gave me my first assignment as a reporter." Betty bent from the waist in order to be invisible in the passenger seat. She'd applied her Tabu perfume before starting the trip to New Orleans, and now she wondered if Sam noticed the scent.

His features were indistinguishable in the darkness, but his smooth, even breathing comforted her inner turmoil.

She kept her voice low. "Think you're the Sam Parker named in the letter?"

"Could be. It's my name, my military group, my hometown; but I never expected to receive a gift on the Merci Train." The husky timber of his voice appealed to her.

18

"Sounds like you performed a courageous deed in France, too." She flirted. "Want to tell me?"

Betty touched his arm to encourage him to speak, but jerked back when she felt a shock, exactly like the sensation she'd experienced when she'd pulled the lamp cord out with wet hands.

He winced. Had he felt something too? Then Sam chuckled. "I think you've mistaken me for someone else. I'm not that brave."

Claude rested an arm on the front seat and glanced back at them. "We're out of the French Quarter. You two can sit up now."

Helen spoke, "I'm sorry, Betty, Sam. Some day you'll be able to ride with us without having to duck down for fear of being seen."

Claude snorted and placed his right hand back on the wheel. "My Helen's a dreamer."

"I want to do more than dream, Claude. I want to change things." Helen's words sounded firm.

Betty noted Helen's deliberate movement closer to the passenger door.

Claude blew out a breath. "Not happening, Honey. Think about how *you* changed things. I'm the one doing the work, not you. I convinced the mayor to allow you to start a bookmobile on the other side of the tracks. I got my daddy to hire that colored gal in the mail room of the Gazette. Then, you pushed me to ask my old man to assign her a story. Now, I'm acting as a chauffeur for the likes of them. You haven't changed anything."

"But I'm trying." Helen moved so that she faced Betty and Sam. "Betty's article is about the Merci Train. Maybe you could tell her some of the details you learned today."

Helen's prodding reminded Betty of the task she'd forgotten as soon as she'd viewed Sam's courageous act. "Oh, yes, did you learn anything I could put in my story?"

Sam rubbed his chin. "Before the mayor spoke, the woman in charge of distributing the gifts mentioned items they expected to be in the crates. She said there should be vases, dolls, ashtrays decorated with bullets, drawings from school children, bottles of wine, war medals from the French, several oil paintings. Oh, she was very excited about a wedding dress."

"The French sent a wedding dress?" Betty moved a little closer to him.

"Yes. The woman said that it would require a contest to see who should receive the bridal gown."

Betty wrinkled her nose. "Like Prince Charming having everyone in the kingdom try on the glass slipper."

Helen's voice sounded from the front. "That would be a great story. Will young ladies try on the gown?"

"Not all. She said the Louisiana wedding dress had been designed for a bride with a twenty-four-inch waist and who stood five foot seven." Sam paused.

Claude Roark tapped Helen. "Sounds exactly like someone I know, if I can convince her to marry me."

Sam snapped his fingers. "Oh, she said anyone meeting those two conditions would have to write an essay about what their fiancé had done during the war.

Her committee would judge the essays, then let the top three contenders try on the gown."

Claude placed a hand on Helen's shoulder. "You'd have a fantastic essay. You could write about your husband dying defending his country, and about my service, too."

"But we're not engaged," Helen protested.

"I'm waiting for your 'yes.' Got my eye on the perfect ring."

Betty hadn't known about Helen's relationship with the Gazette editor's son. Maybe that was how she got the mail room job. Was he the reason she finally got an assignment?

She broke the silence. "I'm a sucker for fairy tales. I like stories with happily ever after endings. Why didn't that lady mention the wedding dress at the ceremony?"

Sam sighed. "Well, the mayor thought the doctor's envelope announcing a surprise personal gift would be more exciting. And he was right."

"Helen, I'd love to see you in the Merci Car wedding dress." Claude wolf-whistled. "I'd like to see you in any wedding dress."

"Claude, you don't agree with my beliefs." Helen sighed.

"I love you, Helen, always have, even before your hubby and I went overseas together. Thought you might learn to love me after he died. I'd do anything to convince you to marry me. You tell me you want something, I'll get it, even if it involves the coloreds."

When Betty gasped, Sam covered Betty's hand with his and squeezed it.

She whispered to him. "Sometimes I wish I could get on a giant bird and fly away, to a different place, a different time."

The very personal conversation in the front seat subsided to strident murmurs shooting back and forth over an invisible line.

Sam lifted Betty's hand to his lips. "We don't live in Utopia. We can leave this place."

She scooted closer to him, careful not to move her hand away from his soft lips. "How?"

"I'm going to medical school in Nashville, Tennessee. I've received preliminary acceptance to Meharry, based on my graduation from Southern this spring." He gazed at the patches of lighted houses. "Don't know if I'll return to Louisiana after I become a doctor."

"But this is your home." She turned her shoulders to face him, keeping her voice quiet, so the couple in the front wouldn't hear their conversation.

"Sometimes people need to create new homes." Sam's words were soft.

"I don't think I could. I love my family, not just my own, but I have a truckload of relatives here, too. Don't you?" Betty wondered if he'd heard or if he was ignoring her.

Finally, he answered. "I do, and they're rooting for me. I'm the first in my family to attend college. And when I received acceptance into med school, you'd have thought I'd been elected President of the United States."

"Guess our families are different." She untangled her fingers from his.

He leaned and whispered in her ear. "Let's see if they are. Come to the Scotlandville church on Main Street this Sunday. Meet my folks."

"If I agreed to visit your church, you wouldn't get just me, you'd get my whole family. Tradition, you know, we worship together every week. Want all eight of us?"

"Yes Ma'am, all eight, and tell them to plan on eating with us after the service. Mama's Sunday dinners are the highlight of everyone's week."

"Couldn't come without bringing something. My mama makes lip-smacking buttermilk pies, and we'll bring a cobbler, too."

Claude's voice broke into their privacy. "Nearing Scotlandville, where should I drop you?"

"By the entrance to Southern University, if that's not an inconvenience, Sir. It's straight ahead, Mr. Roark." Sam turned back to her. "See you on Sunday?"

"Definitely." She offered her hand for an agreement shake, but he kissed it instead. The butterflies swarmed in her stomach, and she felt her neck warming.

The car stopped. Helen placed her arm on the seat and looked over her shoulder. "We'll take you to your own front door if you want."

"No, Ma'am." Sam had already opened the door. "Thank you for the ride. Nice meeting you. Thanks again, Ma'am, Sir." He then bobbed his head toward Betty.

Helen called to him as he walked into the dark, tree-lined row. "Sam, if you ever need to get in touch, just call the Jolson Library."

"I will, Ma'am".

Betty issued a huge sigh as he disappeared. "Oh, Helen, isn't that Sam Parker handsome? And nice? And brave? And polite? And smart?"

"Yes, Betty, he's all those things." Helen faced front again.

Claude turned the car around and headed away from the road where Sam had departed with Betty's heart.

Betty inched forward. "Did you love your husband so terribly that it hurt inside?" Betty bit her lip and yelped, when realizing her mistake. "I'm sorry for stepping out of my place, Mrs. Warren. I shouldn't have mentioned your husband."

"It's all right. Sometimes, I don't think about him for days, even weeks. Maybe someday, I'll be able to think of a life without him, but not yet." Helen appeared to be speaking to Claude, not her.

Betty didn't know whether to talk or shut up. She spoke. "I bet you'll love someone else, some day."

"I hope so. My husband's death changed me. I see life differently now. His letters altered the way I feel about things. He wrote how the colored soldiers were treated, men who served as loyally, as bravely as the white soldiers. Opened my eyes to the way things are here in the south. I'd need to find a man who could understand how important equality is to me."

24

Betty sensed the tension in the front seat and noted Claude's hands tighten on the steering wheel. "I bet you'll find that man very soon." Betty sat back in her seat and stared into the darkness.

"That man is sitting right here, Helen." Claude spoke softly, but Betty could still hear him.

She hummed to herself, hoping to drown out their conversation, but the words drifted over the seat and pounced on her dreams.

She tried to focus on the hymn's words, but heard Claude's instead. "Helen, I do understand. Didn't I get Betty her job? Didn't I lobby Dad to let her write a story? Didn't I consent to drive her to New Orleans? What more can I do?"

"You're doing it for me, not because you share my belief."

"That should be more convincing of my affection. I'm willing to do those things, even though I don't share your principles."

Helen dabbed at her eyes with a handkerchief. "That's the problem. I want to marry a man who shares my beliefs."

"But I'm willing to allow you to pursue your beliefs because I love you. I've always loved you, even when I acted as the best man in your wedding ceremony. I watched you marry another, when you were the one I loved."

The car slowed to a crawl. Betty stopped humming and began singing one of last Sunday's selections, *Standing on the Promises*. She didn't want them to think she was nosey. By the time she'd finished three stanzas, the couple in the front was quiet. Silence cloaked the sedan.

Betty twisted the cotton fabric of her skirt, and broke the stillness. "Helen, I'll always be grateful to you for starting the bookmobile for our side of the tracks. All the little kids look forward to Tuesday afternoons."

Helen looked over the seat. "I hope the bookmobile will continue after I leave."

"Oh, Ma'am, you can't leave the bookmobile. You are the bookmobile."

"I've mourned my husband for four years. I'm ready for a new start, in a new place, not this suffocating community." Helen gazed at Claude.

"I couldn't imagine leaving home, starting over." A horrible and selfish thought crept into Betty's mind. When Helen left, Betty's life would fall back into the crevices of darkness. Helen had been her mentor, her supporter.

As if reading her mind, Helen turned to her. "Betty, you're braver and smarter than you realize. Tell Claude your address, so we can get you home."

"One, one, uh, one, two," Betty stuttered.

"One, one, uh, one, what kind of address is that?" Claude turned toward Helen. "And this is the gal you thought could write a newspaper article?"

"My address is one, two, seven, three Maple Street." Betty enunciated carefully. "But you can drop me at the corner. Maple is a dead-end."

"Dead end? How suitable!"

Helen peered over the seat. "Betty, would you like to come to my house for coffee on Sunday afternoon?"

"Thank you for the offer, Mrs. Warren, but I have other plans on Sunday—with Sam." She felt the skin stretch with the wideness of her grin.

"It's Helen. All my friends call me Helen, and I count you as one of them. If you want to show me your newspaper article before you turn it in, I'd be happy to read it. But I know your writing, you can turn it in without an extra set of eyes."

The warmth in Helen's voice convinced Betty of her sincerity. She hoped her *friend* would not link her life to Claude Roark's. Betty longed to give Mrs. Warren a comforting hug, but that would be inappropriate.

When Claude slammed on the brakes, Betty lurched forward and back. "Here you go, Miss Reporter. Now, my sweetie and I can go have some fun."

Betty tried to see her home through the eyes of Claude and Helen. She didn't think either of them could possibly understand the wealth of love that existed inside those four walls.

Could she ever consider leaving this place as Helen planned to do? As Sam intended to do?

Chapter 4

Sam doggedly pursued his studies, but sometimes his mind wandered, lighting on a young lady named Betty Jackson with striking brown eyes and a voice that rivalled the singing of birds. When this happened, he lost track of time. After one bout of whimsy, he realized he'd been woolgathering for an hour as the clock's minute hand had marched a complete circle. He shoved his chair under the desk and sprinted to his job at the local po'boy spot favored by college students.

Tomorrow would be Sunday, and his parents would meet her for the first time. He'd never brought a girl home they didn't know. His parents had known all the ladies in this community close to his age.

And he'd be meeting her family, too. Would they like him?

At the sandwich shop, he stowed his books, slipped on a red apron embellished with Zack's Genuine Louisiana Po'boys, and clocked in with a wave to the owner.

"Oh, Sam, feller came in here looking for you. Said he'd meet you at closing."

"You didn't know him?" Sam checked the clipped papers on the wire and began slicing roast beef.

"Nope. Said you would, though. Said his name was Burton."

Sam swallowed. Burton. What was he doing here in Scotlandville? Burton's journey to this black college town was not accidental. He'd blamed Sam for his friend's knife wound. Sam closed his eyes and prayed that Burton's visit meant that Sanford Dickens had lived, not died.

His shift moved with molasses-pouring slowness, and he previewed Burton's future visit through his mind in newsreel fashion, with a different clip each time. Sam considered himself an optimist, but today, only a few of his imaginings ended happily.

How would he get to Nashville? Pay for room, board, tuition, and books at Meharry? And how would he stay alive until he graduated? Tonight's dilemma was avoiding a confrontation with Burton.

At closing time, Sam glanced out the window. No Burton. Well, he wasn't peering in the windows, and there was no car directly in front of the cafe.

The owner switched the open sign to closed, pulled the shades, and locked the front door. Together, they balanced the register, cleaned the kitchen, restocked the napkin holders, and replenished the café's original hot sauce containers.

"See you tomorrow, Sam." The owner, with the huge belly, flipped off the light switch and held the door.

"Not tomorrow, that's Sunday, but I will see you Monday."

"Monday, it is. You college boys are too smart for me." The man cuffed him playfully on the chin and walked into the darkness.

29

Sam checked left and right. No Burton. How had the man found him? The letter read during the Merci Train ceremony mentioned Scotlandville, but not where Sam worked. And why had he come?

Turning up his collar against the evening chill, Sam judged the number of steps to the corner and began counting. He needed the distraction to take his mind off Burton's visit to the sandwich shop.

The leaves rustled. Not much light, even though there was a half moon. He stopped and listened. Had he heard steps behind him? Nobody in sight. Maybe Burton was waiting at his home. If he'd discovered where Sam worked, he probably knew where he lived. That thought spurred him into a run.

He'd adapted a steady stride when the car pulled next to him, matching his speed.

"Evening, Sam. Let me give you a ride." Burton steered the car off the road and into the beaten path which served as a sidewalk.

Why was this happening to him? Sam didn't bother turning to sprint in the opposite direction. Burton drove while Sam walked, and he had to face Burton some time.

"Thank you, but I'm not that far from home." Sam lowered his head.

Sam's daddy had emphasized from the time Sam had been old enough to listen that in any encounters with the white folks, he should keep his fists down and his head down.

"Thought you might want to know about Sanford." Burton stepped out of the car.

Sam realized they were near an abandoned house with a yard of discarded tires, an old stove, bags of garbage, broken limbs, and unkempt, overgrown bushes. And he understood why Burton waited to stop him until they arrived at this very spot.

"How's Sanford doing? Did the doctor patch him up?" Sam maintained his position.

If Burton intended to use his fists or his knife on him, Sam had a better chance out here rather than in the shadows behind that empty house.

Your buddy is fine, except in the head." Burton shoved Sam's shoulder. "Says he plans to visit you, thinks you might be friends. I'm his friend, not you. Sanford shouldn't have jumped in front of you. Stupid thing for him to do."

Sam's hands involuntarily clenched into fists, but he kept his thumbs against the seam on his pants. "Is he out of the hospital?"

"What's it to you? Your kind ain't welcome to visit patients in the hospital." Burton circled Sam and came back to face him.

"So Sanford's still in the hospital?" Sam asked.

"Didn't say that, did I?" Burton put a finger under Sam's chin and forced his head up. "And it's Mr. Dickens to you, not Sanford."

A cloud passed over the moon's section, and Sam strained to hear any signs of community life and failed.

Burton shoved Sam again, this time with both hands. "How come a decorated soldier won't fight?"

"No reason to fight you, Sir."

31

"Well, let me give you one." Burton landed a left to Sam's mid-section, followed by a right to the jaw.

Sam concentrated on his family, on Betty, on his future as a doctor, and on his classes as his body received pummeling blows and walloping kicks. Blows hammered at his midsection, and when he fell, he tucked his hands in his armpits. A surgeon needed hands without any broken bones. Burton's shoe struck his ribs. Now, even his breathing hurt. Had Burton cracked some ribs? Broken them? Surely Burton would get tired of hitting him or stop because Sam refused to fight back.

The last thing he recalled was the mournful hoot of an owl returning home from the hunt.

Chapter 5

Betty dabbed the Tabu perfume behind her ears and checked her teeth for traces of lipstick. She looked over her shoulder at her reflection in the mirror. Betty usually rotated her three Sunday dresses for church, but today, she decided on the red gabardine. Satisfied with her look, front and back, she clapped a red hat on her head and used a hatpin to secure it. She clipped on black earrings and stepped into her pumps. Betty wanted to look her best, since their first meeting had been in the back seat of a car and in semi-darkness.

"Betty, quit admiring yourself and get down here." Her daddy's crustiness hid a loving, gentle heart. "You can ride in the cab with me and your mother if you can keep your feet out of the cobbler and balance the buttermilk pies on your lap. We'll put the rest of the kids in the back."

Betty hurried into the kitchen. "Oh, thank you, Daddy. I didn't want my hair messed up."

Her father looked perplexed. "Don't think that hair would dare move. You've got enough spray for a whole Sunday School class on that head of yours."

"Oh, Daddy. Be serious. Do I look all right?" She turned around in a slow circle so he could see her from all sides.

"You look pretty as a sunrise. My interest today is the young man who thinks he might be worthy of my Betty." Her father patted her on the back. "You'll take his breath away, Miss Sunshine. I almost feel sorry for the feller. He doesn't have a chance."

Betty grabbed a peppermint from the dish by the door to sweeten her mouth and settle her jittery stomach. Then they were on their way to meet Sam and his family.

When Betty's family rolled into the lot in their coughing, wheezing pick-up, she saw a man standing by the church's white painted entry. Sam!

But this was not the Sam she'd seen in New Orleans last Sunday saving a man's life. Could he be the man who kissed her hand, told her his plans to become a doctor, and wanted their families to meet?

Her daddy shut off the engine and pulled on the brake. "That the fellow you dressed up for?"

Betty stared at Sam. What had happened to him? His whole face was swollen, a big lump on his chin and his left arm in a sling testified to a serious scrap.

Her daddy clicked his tongue. "Looks like a brawler to me. You don't want to get involved with any short-tempered man who does his talking with his fists. Maybe we should go back home."

"Please let him explain." Betty slid to the side of the seat, placed the pies where she'd been sitting, and rushed to Sam.

Her mother helped the other children out of the pick-up bed, and when she'd lined them up like soldiers, she linked arms with Betty's father. The Jackson family marched toward the sanctuary. Her father nodded slightly toward her and Sam. Betty thought he looked at Sam's disfigured face with disapproval, not sympathy.

* * *

Betty and Sam offered to walk home and set the table while the Jackson family and the Parker family paid their compliments to the preacher and rounded up the children.

Betty gently tapped Sam's forehead above his right eye which was puffy and almost closed. "You look different. Can't put my finger on it, but different. Want to tell me what happened?"

"No. No reason for you to know." He tucked her hand into the crook of his arm. "May not look good, but I feel like a millionaire with a stunning woman on my arm."

"My daddy thought you were fighting."

"I was attacked, but I didn't fight back." His words emerged crisp and brittle.

"Thought you should know that my daddy will ask, even if we are guests in your home." She shivered as a cold breeze shook the trees along their path and freed some leaves for sailing. "Won't you tell me what happened?"

"Betty, it's best if you stay out of it. I wanted you to come today, but I shouldn't have asked. I spend most of my days and some nights in class or studying. When I'm not on campus, I'm working. I hold down two jobs and rarely have a free minute."

"You sound like a very busy man. Are you too busy to go for a walk or catch a movie or get a malt?"

"Maybe. I've decided to try to finish my classes early. I'm talking to the dean tomorrow."

"This eagerness to leave home wouldn't have anything to do with your new look, would it?" She angled her head and held the pose.

"Betty, I don't want to be too busy for getting to know you, but..." He motioned toward a small green-painted house. "This is our place."

She stopped by the picket fence. "We don't have to stay for Sunday dinner."

"Please do." He opened the clasp on the gate and held it for her to enter. "We'll talk, later."

Inside, Betty noticed the crisp white tablecloth and the brilliant-colored leaves in a flower bowl on the dining room table. Sam's mother might have been eager to make a good impression, too.

What was he hiding? He remained silent as he handed Betty the plates stacked on the kitchen counter and counted silverware.

"How many places?" Betty evaluated the table's capacity.

"Eight of you, seven of us. Fifteen, total, but my youngest sister will end up in Daddy's lap, so put two plates in his spot at the head of the table."

"My little brothers wouldn't mind eating on the porch." Betty arranged plates on the long table which would not accommodate fourteen.

"I'll get the card table." He handed her the forks and knives and retreated to another room.

She heard her family's rattling pick-up before the clatter and chatter of voices overwhelmed the quiet.

Mrs. Parker hustled into the kitchen and donned an apron. She stirred pots and removed the meatloaf from the oven, and directed the younger ones to pour tea into glasses.

Betty observed her father and Mr. Parker talking amiably. They joked about her family's unreliable pick-up, while Mr. Parker matched stories with tales about his unpredictable sedan. If her daddy had asked Sam's father about Sam's appearance, he'd apparently been satisfied.

But Betty wasn't. She'd need to use her reporter skills to get some information from Sam Parker.

***

"Dinner was delicious, Mama, but Betty and I want to take a walk before we tackle dessert." Sam wagged a finger toward his younger brothers and sisters. "And you're not coming with us. I'll be escorting Miss Betty by myself. No following us, no popping up in front of us, and no jumping from behind a hiding place and yelling boo."

Mrs. Parker added to Sam's edict. "If you don't leave Sam and Betty alone, you forfeit dessert."

Betty's mom chimed in, "Goes for all you Jacksons, too. You hassle your sister and no treats for you."

Betty sniggered. "Our mamas just gave us an hour of freedom."

"Let's not waste a second." Sam tugged at her hand, leading her down the porch steps.

She gushed with the information she'd bottled up. "I'm going back to New Orleans with Helen and Claude on February 25. They're opening the Merci Train crates that day. You should go with us, find out about your special gift from France."

"I'll stay in class. You can accept my present. My guess is that it's from a Dr. LeGrande. I saved his son's life, but the young man will never become a doctor like his father. Can't operate with one arm. The LeGrandes invited me to their home for dinner. Can you imagine that happening in Louisiana?" Sam halted in the middle of the path. "Wait. You have a second newspaper assignment?"

"I brought a copy of my first article." She fished in her pocket and presented a small piece of newsprint. "I wrote that, those are my words, and the editor wants me to do a feature about the wedding dress."

"The beginning of your career." Sam pointed down the street to Zack's Genuine Louisiana Po'boys. "That's one of the places I work. Do you think Mrs. Warren will enter an essay for the wedding gown competition?"

"I don't know. Claude Roark really wants to marry her. You heard him talking in the car."

"I know I'm a man, but the lady didn't seem keen on wanting to marry Mr. Roark."

Betty tapped her head. "You're a smart man. After the bookmobile closed on Tuesday, Mrs. Warren offered me a soda. She seemed so sad. She wants to marry again and worries that Claude might be the only one who will ask her. They've been friends a long time. But I don't think she should marry Claude, do you?"

"Not my decision. Nor yours." He lifted her hand to his heart. "Betty, would you write to me? Write something every day and mail it at the end of the week. I want to know everything about you."

"Everything?" Betty offered a quizzical look.

"Everything you want to tell me," he said.

"And will you write back?"

"I will." Sam squeezed her hand. "I think we should just write. I don't think we should see each other."

"Why?"

Sam stared off in the distance. "I never know when some old Army buddy might show up. I wouldn't want one of them to steal my girl."

His comment puzzled her. Why did he say "I don't think we should see each other" in one breath and call her "my girl" in the next?

She prepared a rebuttal. She wanted to see him again, and soon, but the set of his jaw told her that she would not change his mind.

Chapter 6

Sam toed the carpet, eyes down. "Dean Keaton, I have a problem."

"I could tell that by looking at your bruised face. Have a seat." The dean motioned to a winged-back chair. "Now, what can I do for you?"

Sam inhaled deeply and blew the breath out. "For my safety, and my family's, I think I should leave here as soon as possible."

"You're scheduled to graduate in May." The dean eased into the chair behind his desk.

"Could my classes be accelerated? I realize treating my case as special is a big imposition on my professors." Sam paused.

"But?" prompted the dean.

"Although I've been granted acceptance to med school at Meharry, the admission depends on my graduation."

"You've given this some thought before you knocked on my door. What do you have in mind?" The dean searched Sam's face.

"I hoped it might be possible to receive my class assignments for the remainder of the year, complete them, and sit for my exams early." Since the swelling around his eye socket blocked the normal range of his vision,

Sam lifted his chin a little higher in order to see Dean Keaton, gauge his reaction.

"Granting your request would set a precedent." The dean tapped his teeth with his thumbnail. "Have you talked to your parents about your fears for their safety?"

"No, Sir. They're worried about what might happen to me." Sam pursed his lips. "I wanted to talk to you, see if you might agree to my request."

"I'll discuss the matter with your professors and the board." Dean Keaton moved his head side to side. "I wish I could shield all my students, keep them all protected and free from harm, but we have to live in this world, a world that's not always fair."

"I don't think I'm being cowardly, but I am worried about my family, and the safety of a beautiful young lady." Sam sat up straighter. "I'm afraid my adversary might not be content with using me as his only punching bag. If I left, I think he'd consider that as a win and wouldn't take his meanness out on the ones I love."

The dean swiveled his chair around and stared out the window, watching students as they changed classes. "I'll see what I can do. Stop in next week, Sam. I'll try to have an answer for you. Don't get your hopes up."

When Sam reached the door, he heard a muffled moan. Remembering his manners, he turned to extend his thanks but stopped when he saw the dean had dropped his head into his hands and that his shoulders were shaking.

***

41

Sam rummaged through the desk drawer until he found some plain stationary. Betty's letter should be on nice paper, not his blue-lined theme paper. He filled the bladder of his fountain pen and set it aside. He'd asked Betty to write, and he'd promised to reciprocate with a few lines or paragraphs each day. He'd write his message in pencil so he could cross out or change things, then he'd copy his words in pen.

Betty,

I have your newspaper article taped to my desk. When I read it, I think of you. To be truthful, I think of you even when I haven't been near my desk. Are you still going to New Orleans for the opening of the crates this week with Helen? I will scribble a note asking the chairman to allow you or Helen Warren to pick up the "Sam Parker" gift which caused so much consternation at the official ceremony. I'm adding Mrs. Warren's name, in case the person in charge would question entrusting the package to you.

Today I asked the dean if I could accelerate my classes and finish my school year as quickly as possible. You saw my face on Sunday, and I'm worried about the people I love and those I like. I don't want anyone harmed. If I leave, he'll take it as a personal victory. If the university approves my suggestion, my only regret will be not spending more time getting to know you.

Should he tell her everything? No. He should spend his time studying in case the dean approved his idea. He pulled out his calculus book and closed it when something Burton had said flashed into his mind.

Burton said Sanford was alive and fine—except in the head. And the bully never answered the question of whether or not Sanford was still in the hospital. Had there been complications in Sanford's surgery? Had something gone wrong? Was that why Burton paid him a visit?

Sam ransacked his drawers for spare change. Calling the hospital would give him a few answers. He raced to the local drug store and located a booth with a phone book attached to a chain. Hospitals. He used his pen to write the number on his hand and dialed.

"Could you please connect me to the room of Sanford Dickens?"

"We don't have a Sanford Dickens registered."

Sam blew out his breath. "Can you tell me if he's been discharged or was transferred to another hospital? Mr. Dickens was admitted on Sunday, February 13 with a knife wound to the neck."

"Sir, I can only tell you that we don't have anyone by the name of Sanford Dickens in this hospital."

Sam tapped his forehead with the heel of his hand. What was the doctor's name? Sam hadn't waited for the physician to state his name. Sam had been too proud to announce that he would be going to medical school and didn't need an orderly's job.

"May I connect you with anyone else?"

"No, thank you." Sam bounced his head off the back of the phone booth, lined up the remaining coins and looked up Dickens in the phone book. Too many, the number of listings made him chuckle. He'd have a *dickens* of a time finding the right Dickens in New

Orleans, and the Sanford Dickens he wanted might not even live in the city.

Chapter 7

Betty sliced the envelope open with a paring knife. Writing filled two sheets top to bottom, front and back, but the third sheet boasted only a few lines. She read the words aloud.

To Whom It May Concern:

I, Sam Parker of Scotlandville, Louisiana, and a member of the 761st Tank Battalion, request that the package sent for me in the Merci Train car be given to Mrs. Helen Warren or Miss Betty Jackson. The doctor whom I believe wrote the letter and sent the present is Dr. LeGrande, and his son's name is Paul. I confirm that I helped Paul when he was injured and stayed with the young man when the surgeon removed his arm. I also visited the LeGrandes' home which is in Le Havre, France. I hope this is enough information to prove that I am the intended recipient of the gift.

Respectfully,

Samuel Edison Parker

Betty held the sheet to her chest. She repeated his full name, Samuel Edison Parker, liking the way it rolled off her tongue, and how distinguished the parts sounded together. When he earned the title of doctor to put in front of those three names, his personal identification would impress anyone.

She scurried to the room she shared with her sisters, glad they were still in school so she could savor every word written by Mr. Samuel Edison Parker.

After a third reading, she hid her personal letter in her underwear drawer and took the "to whom it may concern" sheet to the library. This February day wore a cloak of gray, and the chilly wind forced Betty to tighten the belt on her jacket. She knocked on the library's heavy oak door, but Helen didn't answer.

"Yes?" The assistant librarian, a rotund man wearing thick, black-rimmed glasses, glared at her.

"May I speak to Mrs. Warren?" Betty peeked around his wide frame to the book-lined interior, hoping to glimpse her friend.

"Mrs. Warren is sick. Are you Betty Jackson?" He examined her through the slight opening he'd allowed, keeping the warmth inside the city building. "Wait here. I have a message for you."

Betty shifted her weight from one foot to the other and rubbed her upper arms with her hands. Why hadn't she worn gloves?

The man cracked open the door and poked an envelope in her direction. "You'd probably be warmer if you read the note at your home."

She ripped open the envelope as soon as he shut the library's door.

Once home, she spotted her daddy bent over the card table searching for two more edge pieces of the 500-piece puzzle featuring a field of flowers. "Glad you're here,

46

Betty. I could use some of your Miss Sunshine magic to discover the fillers for those spots."

Betty spread out the jigsaw cutouts. "I think the one on the side is missing, Daddy. We had this puzzle on the table when everyone came for the Fourth of July. Remember how angry Aunt Sallie was? She'd made finding that piece her mission, and she was boiling mad when it wasn't in the box."

"I do. Your Aunt Sallie has quite a temper and a tongue to go with it, even though she sits on the second pew in church every Sunday." Her daddy sat and crossed his arms. "You're not smiling today. What's wrong? Spit it out."

"I just found out that Helen Warren is sick and won't be taking me to New Orleans for the opening of the Merci Train crates tomorrow."

"Betty, you know I can't take you. Even if we didn't need the pickup here, I'm not sure our bundle of bolts would make the eighty miles to New Orleans." He wiped his face with a handkerchief and grinned. "Then we'd have to turn around and come back."

Betty nodded. "I know. I wasn't asking you to take me, I have a ride with the son of the newspaper editor, Claude Roark. He wants to marry Helen, so he's doing her a favor. He's the one who took us for the Merci Car arrival."

"But Mrs. Warren's not going. You comfortable with that arrangement?"

"I think so."

47

Her daddy tugged at her earlobe. "A 'think so' isn't a yes. You don't have to go. I know you want to see your words in print again, but you'll get more chances."

Betty offered her daddy Sam's single sheet. "I also want to collect Sam's present. His gift shouldn't get lost in the unpacking frenzy."

"You consider yourself a grown woman at nineteen, so you'll make the decision about going off to New Orleans with Mr. Roark." He touched her nose. "But I'm concerned. I'll always see you as my little girl. Are you sure you can trust him?"

Betty flung her arms around his neck, surprised at the tears which filled her eyes. Then she stepped back. "Mr. Roark is in love with Mrs. Warren, he's not interested in me. Daddy, I'm taking my Brownie camera to photograph items from the crates. Maybe the editor will publish one of my pictures for the story I write."

"Maybe he will, Miss Sunshine. Would you look at this?" He held up an edge piece. "You've brought me luck. Now we can start working on this puzzle in earnest. Want to help?"

***

Betty chattered the first fifteen minutes of the ride without encouragement or response from Claude Roark.

"My ears are tired. I'm turning on the radio." Claude twisted the knob and found a jazz station.

Betty strained to read the roadside signs, relieved at the declining number of miles to the destination. He'd assured her he knew the warehouse location.

He maneuvered the red Ford through the back streets, parking in a sparsely occupied lot. "Let's go. Don't need to lose my whole day."

Betty removed the Brownie from her tote bag and snapped pictures of the bleak exterior. One shot captured Mr. Roark grimacing as he motioned for her to follow him.

The Merci Train car with colorful medallions representing the French provinces reposed in splendor in the middle of the warehouse. Where were the people? Had they come on the wrong day? At the wrong time? She padded softly around the perimeter, relieved to hear voices.

The transport's sliding doors, pushed to their limits, stood open and broad wooden steps on the floor provided a stable entry. Lined up outside the car were crates of varied sizes, men with crowbars, a photographer, two stenographers, and the woman who had been introduced as the person in charge of gift distribution.

Mr. Roark cleared his throat and addressed the lady in charge. "Name's Roark. I'm with the Jolson Gazette, and we're here to claim that special package for Sam Parker, the one you mentioned on the day of the Merci Car's arrival." He snapped his fingers in Betty's direction and she produced Sam's precious paper.

"I'd love to free myself of that particular gift." The woman pushed her glasses up on her nose, reading the short note. "But your name is Roark, and this letter says Helen Warren or Betty Jackson."

"Helen Warren is my fiancée, she's sick today. Didn't think you'd mind getting rid of the embarrassing hot potato."

"Not at all. Take both the letter from the French doctor and his gift off my hands." She turned to the men with crowbars. "That's in crate seven. Don't think I'll ever forget that humiliating day. Open it up."

With the contents exposed, she delved through the items until she found the gift marked for Sam Parker and handed it to Claude Roark. She then turned to the stenographer. "Don't record that gift."

"Thanks." Claude nodded to the woman, then thrust the gift and letter toward Betty.

Betty caressed both items before placing them in her tote. She imagined being with Sam when he opened the present from across the ocean.

Claude spoke again, "Hear the Frenchies sent a wedding gown. My fiancée's going to need one, and I might want to put my name on the list for that one."

The woman's face bloomed with excitement. "I'm excited about that gift, too. Let's open that crate first." After checking the French shipping manifest, she directed the men with crowbars to box number eighteen, easy to find since the crates stood in numeric order.

Betty snapped pictures with her Brownie, while the official photographer positioned himself for the best-angled shot.

Betty gasped as the woman stretched her hands above her head to present the magnificent wedding gown for all to view. She motioned with her head for Betty to

50

pull the train part of the dress to its full extent, so she put the Brownie away and lifted the train from the warehouse floor.

Betty had never seen anything so beautiful made by a human being. She ran the material between her fingers, savoring the fabric's richness. The ivory satin brocade pattern featured floral bouquets tied with bows, and Betty wrinkled her nose as she tried to estimate the distance between the end of the train that she held and the body of the long-sleeved gown held by the woman. The train would trail at least six feet behind the bride. What would it be like to wear such a splendid item of clothing?

"Where's that camera?" Claude pawed through Betty's bag. "I'm going to take some pictures to show Helen. That dress could have been made with her in mind. I want Helen to have it."

The woman smiled as she shook her head. "No, we're not giving this away. The inventory sheet says the dress was made for a woman at least five foot seven, with a waist smaller than twenty-four inches. That will eliminate the majority of the women in Louisiana. For those remaining, I've decided to promote an essay contest, open to prospective brides who will marry a man who served in the war."

Claude clicked shot after shot. "My sweetie is the perfect candidate, and she's a librarian, so she will write a great essay."

"I wish your fiancée luck in the competition." The woman turned to Betty. "Girl, fan the train out fully on

51

the floor and then move. I don't want you to be in the photographs."

Betty did as told, then picked up her bag and joined Mr. Roark who stood by the warehouse door, tapping his foot.

He handed her the camera. "That didn't take long. We might still have time for some fun."

Chapter 8

"Zack's Po'boys, this is Sam." He heard labored breathing before the person on the other end of the line spoke.

"Sam Parker? Is it you?"

"Betty?" Even though he'd only known her a short time, he recognized her voice, and his instincts told him something was wrong."

"I have your present from the Merci Train."

He waited for her to continue, but heard nothing. "Betty, are you okay?" A sick feeling doubled him over, and he perched on the stool under the phone on the wall. He remembered how Burton appeared at the sandwich shop. Had Burton found her? "Betty, have you been hurt? Has anyone harmed you?"

Betty's response came out flat, strained, not in her vibrant, roller-coaster speech pattern. "I'm fine, just tired. It's been a long day. I thought you'd want to know that your 'to whom it may concern' letter worked. We should get together, so you can find out what the doctor gave you."

Sam glanced from the phone to the row of waiting orders on the wire string growing ever longer. "Should I walk to your place after work tonight?"

"No!" He heard the panic in her voice. "Sam, you can't go out walking in the middle of the night." She paused. "But I'd like to see you tomorrow."

"I'll see if I can borrow the car and come to your place. How early will you be awake?"

"I'll be awake whenever you arrive. Bye, Sam."

The buzz on the line replaced her voice. Sam jammed the receiver into the cradle and grabbed some orders and sliced open several French loafs and heaped ingredients on the sandwich. She said she'd be awake whenever he arrived which meant she wouldn't be sleeping tonight. The insidious thought, hiding in the shadows, appeared again. Had Burton found her? Worse, had he threatened or harmed her?

"Sam, two orders for our table are wrong. This one should have no lettuce, and I requested heavy sauce, but didn't get any."

"I'll fix them." Sam repaired the sandwiches and handed them to the customer, a friend from his calculus class.

His thoughts interfered with his sandwich making. She'd said not to come to her house tonight. Why hadn't she said what was wrong?

* * *

In the early morning, the soft light dressed the dew on the grass with glistening sparkles. Sam steadied the pedal to maintain the speed limit. His daddy needed the car back by nine. When he arrived, he jerked the emergency brake on, stopping next to the Jackson pickup. Betty appeared on the porch, wrapped in a quilt and holding a steaming mug.

The driver's door always stuck. He pushed on it with his shoulder, but Betty opened the passenger side before he could get out to meet her.

She held out the cup. "Brought you coffee, black with sugar. You like your tea sweet, thought you'd like your coffee the same."

He wrapped the mug in his hands when he really wanted to enfold the bearer in his arms. Her implacable face matched the unremarkable tone of her voice. He knew she would tell him everything, but in her own time. He took a sip, positioned his back against his door so he could watch her and waited.

She shivered and pulled both sides of the quilt tighter. "Chilly this morning."

"Weather will change."

"I forgot your Merci Train gift." She placed her hand on the door handle.

"Later, Betty."

But she raced from the car and returned with a package and the letter that accompanied the present. "Want to open it now?"

"No." He placed the gift in the back seat. "I want to know why you called Zach's last night, why you wanted me to come here early today."

Betty wriggled back into her spot, tugging the quilt up to cover her shoulders. "You know I went to New Orleans yesterday for the official opening of the crates."

He nodded. "With Mrs. Warren and Mr. Roark."

She looked out the passenger window. "Just Mr. Roark."

"Mrs. Warren didn't go with you?" He battled to keep the panic out of his voice.

"She got sick. Sent me a note that Claude Roark had agreed to take me. She wanted me to make sure you got your gift, and wanted me to have a chance at publishing a second story. I took my Brownie." She turned to him and smiled sheepishly. "My daddy warned me about going."

He closed his eyes, struggling to keep his breathing even and his temper under control. "And?"

"And the trip down was fine. We got your gift, and they opened the box with the wedding dress in it." She turned toward him. "Sam, the gown is gorgeous, a brocaded satin. I actually touched it. The lady asked me to stand behind the dress, holding the train."

Betty's exuberance annoyed him. Was this why she encouraged him to come to her as soon as possible, or was she stalling? "You said the trip down was fine. What about the trip home?"

She gazed out the window again. "Mr. Roark said he wanted to get something to eat, so he stopped at this place off the main road. Of course, I waited in the car, and when he came out about an hour later, I smelled liquor on his breath."

Sam grabbed her shoulders, forcing her to face him. "Did he, did he do anything to you?"

"No, not what you're thinking."

56

"He must have done something. You were pretty upset when you called last night." Relief and frustration surged through him. Claude hadn't raped her, but what had that man done to his beautiful Betty?

Betty's hands moved in her lap as if she were washing them. "He drove a little farther down the road. No other cars around, no houses. He pulled me to him with his left arm and placed his right hand on my thigh. Sam, I didn't encourage him."

"Some men don't need any encouragement." Sam breathed deeply. Listen, he told himself. Let her tell her story in her own time, her own way.

Betty pulled herself away and rested her cheek on the window, avoiding Sam's eyes. "He suggested I give him a kiss, a thank-you for his taking me to New Orleans. I refused. I said 'I thought you loved Helen.' And he laughed like I'd told the best joke in the world. Then Claude said, 'I do love Helen. You're not stupid enough to think I might like you?'"

Sam slid across the front seat and took both her busy hands in his. "Was that the end of it?"

"Yes, and no." Betty looked into Sam's eyes. "Mr. Roark said, "Helen will never know about our little adventure, will she?'"

Sam acknowledged the dilemma she'd faced. "Betty, I'm…"

She interrupted. Her words rushed forth as if her body needed to get the poisonous experience out of herself. "I asked Mr. Roark to look at it from my side, to think about what kind of friend I'd be to Helen if I didn't tell her."

Sam glanced at his watch, nearly eight, but he couldn't leave when Betty needed him. Her pain-filled eyes broke his heart.

She continued, "You know what he did, Sam? He said I could tell Helen, my word against his. He said even if Helen did believe me that she would know his messing with a colored girl didn't mean anything. And he kept laughing. Maybe it was the liquor. He didn't hurt me physically, but why are people cruel on purpose?" Her shoulders shook as she cried, softly, then with heart-wrenching sobs. "He treated me like I was nothing, like I'm not even a person, acted like I don't count for anything."

Sam wrapped her in his arms and kissed her gently. "But you're everything to me."

Chapter 9

Betty waved good-bye after Sam promised to come back tomorrow after church. She'd suggested Sam bring his whole family, not bothering to ask her parents. Her mom and dad liked his folks, and she wanted the two families to become better acquainted. She traced her mouth where Sam's lips had touched hers. Pure sweetness.

Talking to Sam helped her realize what she should do, what she'd want a friend to do for her if their situations were reversed. She believed that her friendship with Helen prevented Claude from forcing himself on her. Helen's protective and caring attitude toward Betty determined the outcome of Friday's trip home from New Orleans, not Claude's morals.

She eased the front door closed as her daddy padded into the kitchen.

"Coffee made?" He cocked his head to the side. "And what are you doing up? And why are you wearing a quilt for a coat?"

"Sam came to pick up his Merci Train gift. His family needed the car today, so this was the only time he could visit."

"What was in the package?" Her daddy doctored his coffee with milk and sugar until it was the tan color of creek rocks.

"Oh, I don't know. He didn't open it." She kissed her father's cheek and pulled her quilt tighter. "I'm going to grab another hour of sleep, if I can sneak into our room without waking my sisters."

"You're not fooling anybody. Something's fishy, Miss Sunshine. Sam shows up before the sun to get his gift and then doesn't open it? You know you can tell me anything. You do know that, don't you?"

"I know."

"Sam appears to be a nice enough fellow, but go slow." Her daddy added another bit of sugar to his mug and wagged a finger in her direction. "Don't tell your mother. She's afraid I'll get the diabetes like my sister."

Don't tell Mother.

Don't tell Helen.

Two predicaments, similar, but different. Could tattling prevent the deterioration of her father's health? Would her revelation of Claude's actions save Helen from future unhappiness?

Would sticking her nose into other people's business help or make things worse? She'd sleep on it.

***

As predicted, the Jacksons welcomed a visit from the Parker clan Sunday afternoon, but the whole group ended up elbow-to-elbow inside the house. The late February weather forgot that the paper white narcissus already showed off their spring blossoms, and the chilly weather kept even the most exuberant children inside. In the kitchen, the kids built domino towers or lined them up on the table before tapping them to fall in a row, howling with delight with each collapse of the train.

Betty savored the forced closeness to Sam, who held the Merci Train present, still in its wrapping, on his lap.

Her daddy pointed to the parcel. "We've all heard a lot about this gift from the Frenchman. You brought it with you, so my guess is you plan to open it here."

"Yes, Sir. Is now a good time?"

"Unless you want us all to die of curiosity, I'd say this is the perfect time." Her daddy winked at Betty.

Her heart fluttered. Her daddy liked Sam. She'd always been a daddy's girl, and if he hadn't approved of Sam, she might re-examine the attraction growing within her.

Sam handed the package to Betty and opened the envelope. "I heard the beginning of the letter when I was with the honor guard in New Orleans, but I'd like to read the whole thing."

Betty nudged his ribs. "We'd like to hear, too."

"Of course." Sam coughed, then began. "Honorable Louisiana friends, I send a personal gift to Sam Parker, a soldier who came ashore at Omaha Beach. The young man saved the life of an injured French resistance fighter, one who met the Americans during that bloody battle. Mr. Parker carried the Frenchman to the field hospital where a medic saved the man's life by amputating his left arm.

61

That young man was my son, and I want Sam Parker, of the 761st Tank Battalion and a native of Scotlandville, Louisiana, to receive this gift. I intended to pass this item to my son, but in view of his injury, he plans to do medical research instead of practicing as a physician. A grateful father, Dr. Antoine LeGrande."

Betty exchanged the package for the letter which she returned to its envelope. "Do you need scissors?"

Sam, who tugged on the edge of the sealed paper, nodded. "Might save me some embarrassment when I can't pull the wrapping off."

The kids abandoned their kitchen activities and squeezed into the already-tight circle in the living room.

Sam used the scissors produced to cut through the exterior packaging and then lifted the lid to display cloth wrappings. With deft fingers, he peeled layer after layer finally revealing the prize. "A stethoscope!"

Betty's eyes filled with tears watching the reverence and appreciation shining on Sam's face. "Did the Frenchman know of your plans to become a doctor?"

Sam nodded. "He knew of my dreams, but when I was in France, that seemed like an impossible fantasy."

"Know how to use that thing?" Her daddy asked.

"Doctor in Scotlandville let me practice when I was a kid. He inspired me to consider medicine." Sam placed the tubes into his ears and leaned toward Betty, then reconsidered. "Let me try these out on my baby brother."

All the children lined up for a chance to have their hearts heard and then to hear Sam's heart.

Betty's dad stopped behind her chair and whispered. "Glad he didn't check your heart, probably pounding like a quarterhorse's ticker at the end of a race."

After children and adults finished practicing with Sam's new instrument, Mr. Parker urged the family to load up in the car, creating a flurry of shoving, elbowing, and seat-calling shouts.

Betty waited by the door with Sam. "Thanks for opening the gift here."

He took her hand. "Betty, would you consider going to Nashville with me? We could both start over in a new town. I can't go to medical school here, and there's no future for you in this town either. You said yourself you received the assignment to write those articles because of Helen's intervention. Betty, you're better than a cleaning lady, and that's what happens to most women around here."

She jerked her hand away. "My mother's a cleaning lady. Nothing wrong with it."

Sam sighed. "Nothing at all, but you're smart, you could be so much more. Maybe you could go to college in Nashville. Wouldn't it be fun for the two of us to make a new start in Tennessee?"

"Are you asking me to marry you?"

Sam gulped. "Hadn't thought that far. Marriage is a big step. You know I like you. I've read each of your letters, learned more about you, but marriage? I'm not sure I'm ready for marriage."

She leaned close to his face and hissed, "You're treating me just like Claude did."

"No, I'm not. Betty, I like you. I might even love you."

Betty shook her head. "Your dad's honking the horn. You'd better go. Good luck with your life in Nashville."

Chapter 10

Sam placed the stethoscope on the shelf above his study desk and plowed through his course material. He read ahead in each subject, preparing himself in case the university gave the okay to his proposal. Dean Keaton reset the appointment from Monday until Thursday, which he considered a good sign.

Sam's mom tapped on his door before opening it a crack. "I'm scrambling eggs, you want some?"

"You bet." His stomach growled and he banged his toe on the bedframe in his haste to follow her. He hopped around on one leg, muttering words not acceptable for a lady to hear.

His mother indicated the empty plates on the counter. "Saw your light on before five. Grits are ready. Dish some up for both of us."

Sam wolfed down the eggs, grits, and toast, knowing his breakfast would have a price. He wiped his mouth and started to rise, but his mother pressed on his shoulder, indicating she had something to say, and that he would listen.

"Dean Keaton asked us to join you for a meeting Thursday at noon. The dean set the time so your daddy

65

and I could both be there. He asked the name of your girl, too. Said he wanted to get in touch with her. I gave him Betty's name and phone number. You know what it's about?"

"No." He'd expected a grilling from his mom about his relationship with Betty, but this topic puzzled him. "I asked for a chance to speed up my course work so I could settle in Nashville before starting school. Wanted time to find a place to stay, get a job, become familiar with the campus, even get some of my textbooks, and start studying."

"So you're eager for us to be in your rear view mirror?" His mother picked up his chipped plate with the floral pattern rimmed in blue.

"That's not it." He scraped the crumbs off the table with his hand and dropped them into the sink.

"Then what is *it*?"

He leaned his hips against the counter and watched her concentrate on the dishes in the sink. "Mama, I thought you'd be safer if I left, I mean our whole family, not just you. I also thought Betty might be safer if I left. And, truth be told, I want to leave. I've been looking over my shoulder for the past several weeks. I'm concerned the man who beat me up might return."

His mom nodded her head slowly, wiped her hands on the dishtowel and draped it through the oven handle. "Well, I don't think Dean Keaton would schedule a meeting with us and your Betty to say you could finish early."

"Neither do I. We'll have to wait until Thursday to see what Dean Keaton has up his sleeve. Thanks for breakfast, Mama."

* * *

Sam's parents, in their Sunday finery, sat in straight-backed chairs outside the dean's office. He checked the hall clock as Betty and Helen Warren walked down the tile hallway, their high heels sounding a castanet rhythm. Five minutes before noon. Did everyone know what this meeting concerned except him?

Dean Keaton opened his office door promptly at twelve and stood back so all could enter. Sam took the last position, and the first face he saw inside the office was that of Sanford Dickens, paler and thinner, but alive. And the man's eyes gleamed with intelligence, a relief to Sam because Burton's statement about Sanford's being not quite right in the head had haunted him.

Sanford crossed the room and pumped Sam's hand while the Dean seated the guests. "Sam Parker, I'm so glad to see you. The doctor says I'll be good as new, thanks to your quick action. Come sit next to me. We have some business to conduct."

Sam quickly gauged Sanford's appearance. His steady gait, lack of tremors, and clear, focused scrutiny indicated there had been no physical or mental damage due to loss of blood flow.

The dean made introductions, then nodded to Sanford who edged to the front of his chair, eager to address the group.

"Doctor told me I had to remain on bed rest for three weeks, so I assigned my mother the task of tracking you down. She's better than Nick and Nora Charles together." Sanford smiled at Mrs. Parker. "Bet you're good at detective work, too."

Sam's mother beamed. "God gives that talent to mothers."

"Burton Loughman, my good friend, drove me here…"

Sanford's words receded into the background as Sam saw Burton emerge from the back of the room, holding a soda can.

The dean hadn't included Burton in the round of niceties and apologized to the group. "Please forgive me, Mr. Loughman. Let me start over."

"No need. I heard everyone's moniker." Burton's placid expression perplexed Sam. "Go on with your speech, Sanford."

Sanford did. "Sam, I came here today to present you with a reward, actually it's from my parents. They think their only son's life is worth quite a bit. I made it through the war, including Omaha Beach, and survived a peace-time injury, due to your quick and efficient action." Sanford removed an envelope from his jacket pocket and passed it to Sam.

"Sir, I…" Sam tried to stop him.

"Sanford, not 'sir,' and don't refuse my parents this pleasure." Sanford bumped the envelope on Sam's hands which remained palms down.

THE MERCI TRAIN WEDDING DRESS

"I did what any man would do. I shouldn't be rewarded for helping someone in trouble." Sam shook his head.

Betty spoke, "Plenty of men there that Sunday, and Sam was the only one who did anything. Isn't that right, Helen?"

Betty turned to her friend for confirmation.

"That's true, Mr. Dickens. I was with my friend Betty in New Orleans for the Merci Car arrival, and we saw everything. No one tried to help, except Sam." Helen patted Betty's hand reassuringly.

Sanford tugged down his shirt collar to expose his scar. "The man who sewed my throat closed said you wanted to become a doctor, Sam. Open the envelope. The compensation for saving my life will help you achieve that goal."

"I only did what was right."

Sanford shook his head. "The recipient on the check is blank, but my parents have mentally removed the money from their account. I'm not taking it back."

Sam held up his hands. "Thank your parents for me. I appreciate what they want to do, but I can't take the money."

"My life's been a blur." Sanford leaned back, still holding the envelope. "I'd like to hear what you remember about that day."

Sam looked from Sanford to the man who'd beaten him. "What did Burton tell you?"

"Well, Burton said someone charged from the crowd wielding a knife. He said that man yelled about your being unfit to march with the honor guard, and that everything happened in the blink of an eye. Burton said he tried to protect you and swung at the belligerent man. Fortunately, you'd seen the maniac coming, and jumped to the side. The man knifed me, but by mistake."

"That's a good story." Sam looked at Burton who nodded.

Sanford waved the envelope again. "The doctor said you stopped the bleeding by applying pressure to my neck. Said you went all the way to the hospital, never removing your hands. According to him, your quick actions saved me. Please accept this check as an appreciation token for the gift of my life."

Sam smiled. "To see you alive and well is reward enough."

The dean cleared his throat. "Do we have an impasse?"

"I'm not leaving here with this check." Sanford stretched the offering toward Sam.

Sam held up his hand, indicating for Sanford to stop pressing the issue. "I wouldn't feel right accepting the money.

Dean Keaton intercepted the envelope. "I'm a college administrator. I have no trouble accepting money or funneling it in the right direction. Mr. Dickens, I have an idea about how to disburse this money in a way that will satisfy you and your parents' desire to reward Sam. Give me your address and I'll share my plan with you, before I cash the check and implement it."

"Satisfactory to me. How about you, Sam?"

Sam noted the disappointment in the set of his parents' shoulders. "Taking the money would be against the principles you've taught me." He turned to Sanford. "I'm happy for the money to go to Southern University."

Dean Keaton stood, signifying the meeting's end. "I appreciate your trust, both of you."

Sanford shook hands with Mr. and Mrs. Parker, then placed a hand on Sam's shoulder. "You won't accept my money, but would your pride allow me to buy lunch for everyone? I'm starving. Aren't you?"

Sam's parents demurred, citing the need to return to work.

Sam bit his lip. "I'm not sure where we could all go."

Burton stepped up. "You work in a sandwich shop, don't you? Maybe we could get some po'boys to go."

Helen nudged Betty, but directed her comment in Sanford's direction. "I haven't had a shrimp po-boy in a couple of months. I'd love one."

Sam might be a man, but he recognized the interest in Helen's bright eyes when she looked in Sanford's direction.

"Perfect," Betty agreed.

Sam led them through the office door held open by the dean's secretary.

Chapter 11

Betty slid onto the passenger seat of Claude Roark's car which Helen borrowed for the drive to Southern University. The creases in the leather seats, the shiny door handles, and the smell of the interior all made her feel queasy. "Could we ask Sam to ride with us?"

"Of course." Helen waved. "Sam, come in our car. You'll have to show us the way."

After Sam closed the door, Betty turned. "Think your boss will let a mixed group sit at the same table? I guess we could split up. Helen could sit with Sanford and Burton."

The brakes screeched when Helen made a sharp right after Sam's late hand signal. She said, "I think Sanford wants us all to have a meal together."

"Sam, how about your church? Aren't there tables outside?" Betty asked.

"Sure, but is the weather too chilly for you ladies?"

Helen quashed Sam's concern. "A picnic! Great idea!" Helen's voice seemed an octave higher to Betty.

"This is the place, Zach's Genuine Louisiana Po'boys. Why don't we park on the street since we're taking the sandwiches with us? Not many spaces for customers." Sam joined Sanford who waited next to the car.

When the two men returned with several bags, they drove to the Baptist Church, where the two couples spilled out into the crisp March sunshine.

Betty edged next to Sam. "Burton's not eating with us?"

"No," Sam said quietly. "He asked Sanford to buy him a six-pack and cigarettes. Don't think he wants to share our meal."

"Sam, why didn't you tell Sanford the truth about what happened? Burton's story was nothing but a full-blown lie."

"No point. That day in New Orleans, Sanford said he and Burton had grown up together. No reason to destroy a friendship. The past is the past. Let's join Helen and Sanford."

Helen conducted an energetic conversation with Sanford who dispensed sandwiches and drinks.

"I need to get my notebook." Betty raced back to the car and placed the spiral on the table before unwrapping her sandwich.

Helen touched Sanford's mouth with her napkin and laughed. "Sauce is good, isn't it?"

Sanford ran his tongue around his mouth. "The best. This is delicious. I may have to come back once a week. My mother wants me to gain weight."

"You saw the owner, didn't you?" Sam asked.

Sanford laughed. "I'm not sure she wants me to put on that many pounds."

Betty closed her eyes, letting the smell of fresh, damp earth, the light tickle of a breeze on her face and the sounds of songbirds fill her with pleasure. She listened to the ebb and flow of a spirited, cheerful conversation, one which couldn't happen inside a café, in a library, or in any public building.

Helen poked her. "Hey, better open your eyes. Sanford and Sam still look hungry and both are eyeing your po'boy."

"Oh, no. I'm not sharing." Betty created a barrier on the table with her right arm, guarding her lunch from the two men across the table.

"Our Betty wants to be a reporter. That's why she ran off to get her spiral. I'm sure she'll have a long list of questions for Sanford when she finishes her sandwich." Helen bumped Betty's shoulder. "Her latest piece for the Jolson Gazette was about the Merci Train wedding dress."

Sam whistled. "You got the wedding dress article published?"

"Yes, and they used my pictures, too."

Sanford requested and received information about the wedding dress and the essay contest, then he turned to Sam. "You're smart to choose a working woman. She can help you get through medical school, unless you choose to accept my parents' money." Sanford rolled his sandwich paper into a ball and stuffed it in the paper bag.

"Sam's not choosing anyone. He's not ready for marriage." Betty's remark quelled the good-natured banter.

Sam shook his head. "Sanford, you're trying to get me in hot water with that kind of talk."

Helen turned to the man across from her. "Sanford, tell us what's in your future."

Sanford glanced at Betty before speaking. "My enforced rest gave me some thinking time. I earned a business degree before my stint in the Army, but now I'm not sure what I want to do."

Betty examined the curiosity on Helen's face. Her friend liked Sanford. Betty did, too, but Helen liked him in the romantic way. Helen's concern and care for Sanford permeated the air around her. Her friend leaned forward on her elbows, eager to hear the man's every word.

Sanford continued. "I waited around for lightning to strike, a sign of what I should do. War is hell, excuse my language, but the horrors I witnessed changed me. Now I want to do something meaningful with my life, just don't know what. I'm not cut out for a medical life like our friend here. My daddy's a judge. He'd be mighty proud if I rehung the Dickens Law Office shingle."

"You'd have to go to law school," Helen said.

"I would. Do you know any woman who might want to support and encourage me while I get my degree? I was thinking about someone to help me with my law research." Sanford raised his eyebrows.

Betty leaned her head toward Helen. "A librarian would be perfect."

Burton honked the horn four times.

75

"My driver's impatient. Well, I guess I'll be heading home. When can we do this again?" Sanford looked around the picnic table, ending with Betty, instead of Helen.

"You should just visit Helen." Betty folded her sandwich paper, creasing each fold.

Helen placed her hand on Betty's. "All four of us could meet at my little house for a meal. Sanford, we have a Thursday night discussion group at the library. I'd love for you to come and talk to the group about your war experiences."

"Be happy to come to dinner, but I don't do war talks. Sam probably feels the same. Too many good men buried in France."

Burton beeped the horn again, this time ending with one long sound.

"Betty, could you give me a piece of paper? I'd like to get Helen's phone number, if she's willing."

Betty glanced at Helen's glowing face. "I think Helen's willing."

Helen nodded. "Oh, I have another idea. We'll have dinner and then jointly write an essay for the wedding train dress. Wouldn't that be fun?"

"I'm good for dinner. How about you, Sam?" Sanford bumped Sam's shoulder. "We can eat, then let the librarian and the reporter write."

"I'm not certain a group effort would qualify," Betty said.

"Oh, Betty, it's just an excuse to get together. Please say yes," Helen pleaded.

76

Betty nodded as Burton's insistent horn honking assailed the air again.

Sam grabbed Betty's hand before she left with Helen. "Betty, you misunderstood some things I said. Won't you keep on writing to me? I treasure your letters."

The songbirds warbled their melodies so optimistically that Betty squeezed Sam's hand and agreed.

Chapter 12

The following Wednesday Sam returned to Dean Keaton's office and its aroma of lemony furniture polish and old, musty books. Several volumes, opened and closed, covered an alcove desk hidden behind a large hanging spider plant. Sam guessed the secretary positioned the greenery to obstruct any visitor's view of the messy work station.

The dean sported a broad smile, betraying the gap between his two front teeth. "I have an answer to your question. By the way, I enjoyed meeting your friends and your lovely fiancée."

"Uh, no. Betty's not...We are not engaged," Sam sputtered.

"Really? Your mother gave me her name, said Betty would want to come to what I thought was going to be a big celebration. I made the assumption."

"You're not the only person." Sam accepted the seat offered while thinking the dean, his parents, Sanford, and Helen, all tried to promote Betty from friend to future bride.

"Individual study the rest of the year has been approved." The dean tapped several hefty folders on his desk corner.

"I don't feel in as much danger now." Sam ran his fingers around the welting on the chair cushion.

"Any danger is too much. The decision rests with you. I even looked into stops for lodging and food between here and Nashville. Can't be too careful on the road. The places I suggested are safe." He placed an envelope labeled SAM PARKER on the academic binders.

"I'm very appreciative, Sir." Sam studied the pattern in the rug. Should he take the classwork? Refuse it? Gathering materials from his professors cost Dean Keaton time and energy. What should he do? Burton ignored him last week, but Sam's life experiences warned him to remain wary.

When Sam started to speak, the dean shook his head. "Sam, I acted on your proposal for an early departure from campus. Now, please listen to my proposal, with open ears and heart."

"I'll listen." Sam sank back into his chair. He'd prayed to get his assignments and go. Now, he'd be stuck arguing about the acceptance of money for simply doing a good deed.

"I've proposed using the Dickens' money to create a scholarship fund for a Southern University graduate who does advanced study in the field of medicine."

"And I would be the recipient?" Sam laughed. "No disrespect, Sir, but how is that not like accepting a payment?"

"Because we'll attach strings, which I hope will satisfy you. As beneficiary, you receive three hundred dollars for the first year. If you maintain a B average or above in your medical school classes, you could request

79

a similar stipend for the next year, and the next. If you did not succeed, or if you changed your field of study, the money would remain at Southern and go to a different graduate."

"Did the Dickens family agree?"

"They did. Their son Sanford assured them that you wouldn't give up on your plan to become a doctor. He also believes you'll achieve an A average. And I agree."

Sam sighed. "Three hundred dollars is a lot of money. I'd be able to study without holding two additional jobs, but somehow it still seems wrong."

The dean held up a finger. "Oh, Sanford suggested we might send the money to the medical school on your behalf, then you don't accept any money, you just use a scholarship stipend." The dean laughed. "Technicality, but does that work for you?"

Sam studied his hands. "The money would be a blessing. May I add a condition of my own? I'd like for the Dickens money to go on helping medical students. I'll accept on the condition that I pay the money back into the university scholarship fund within five years of receiving my degree. I should make more than twenty-five cents an hour plus tips when I'm a doctor."

"That's up to you, Sam." The dean slid him a single sheet. "Here is the scholarship application form. Just happened to have one handy."

Sam allowed the relief to flood over him. Wouldn't it be wonderful to devote his time to study? And with his part of the proposal, some other student would sit in this chair some day and feel the same sense of liberation.

* * *

A message waiting at the sandwich shop told Sam that dinner and essay writing had been set for Friday at seven and that Sanford would drive him and Betty home that night. Sanford and Helen treated him and Betty in a friendly manner, but what would her neighbors think when a black couple showed up on Helen's front porch. Maybe they should use the back door. Time to think about that later.

The note gave no suggestion that he confirm, just a date and time with the expectation that he'd show. This 'girlfriend' thing annoyed him. Terrified him. He'd been smitten by Betty the first time he saw her. He liked her. He'd invited her family to come to his church and stay for dinner. He liked writing letters and receiving them. He enjoyed learning more about her and spending time with her, but marriage? Would he be slipping into a trap by continuing to date her? Were they dating?

Sam turned to his boss who sliced tomatoes by pressuring them toward the whirring blade, careful to avoid nicking his fingers. "Could I have Friday night off if Jasper can switch with me?"

The sub shop owner never looked away from the machine. "You and Jasper work it out, just don't leave me by myself on a Friday night."

Sam slipped his apron over his head. How could he be happy and mad at the same time?

* * *

On Friday, his mother packaged two loaves of homemade bread and a canning jar with a blooming African violet for him to give Helen as a thank-you gift for the dinner invitation. The six-mile trip to Betty's took his long legs, moving at a clipped pace, over two hours. Despite the cool air, he wiped the perspiration from his brow before knocking on Betty's door.

Seeing her made him forget his tiredness or irritation about her being his girlfriend. She wore a navy polka dot dress trimmed with a white collar and a string of pearls at her throat. She looked stunning. Maybe he did want to marry her.

"Come on in. I made an apple cobbler. Just came out of the oven. I'll have to wrap it up so I won't burn my hands."

"I don't want you to burn your hands." What a dumb thing to say. Had he just repeated what she'd said? What was wrong with him?

Betty's dad insisted on driving them over the tracks to the address Helen had given Betty.

Helen and Sanford opened the front door before Mr. Jackson turned off the ignition, no chance to go around to the back. Sam thought they looked like a happily married couple standing there in the doorway, ready to greet company. Sam glanced around for people on the street or open curtains. He didn't want Helen's neighbors to see that her visitors were black.

Chapter 13

Betty sniffed and smiled at Helen. "Smells good in here. I brought apple cobbler for dessert. It's Aunt Melba's recipe."

Sanford intercepted the wrapped baking dish and lifted the cloth off the corner. "Could we have dessert first?"

Helen wagged her finger. "Now you know that you have to eat all your dinner or you won't get any dessert."

Sanford dropped his head in a pretend pout before looking at Sam. "And what do we have here?"

"My mother's bread and a flower for Helen."

"How kind. I'll put the African violet on my window sill. It's beautiful. I hope I don't kill it. I don't have much of a green thumb. But if I think it's getting sick, I'll call a doctor, or a future doctor." She winked at Sam. "Sanford, don't you dare sneak a bite of that cobbler. You and Sam go in the living room. We'll bring out snacks."

Betty followed Helen into the kitchen, carrying the bread Sam passed to her. "Helen, may I help with dinner?"

Helen laughed gaily. "No, it's done. We're having beef burgundy, noodles, and a Jell-O salad. Can't mess that up. I did the appetizers this afternoon." Helen removed the deviled eggs sprinkled with paprika, shrimp hanging on the lip of a small bowl, and a cheese ball rolled in nuts from the refrigerator. "You can put the crackers on the plate. I'm not sure I'd be able to line them up straight. Oh, Betty, isn't this going to be the best evening ever?"

Sanford and Sam stood when the two ladies came into the living room bearing the snacks and Sanford laughed. "Guess both our mamas taught us to stand for the ladies."

Sam nodded "Mine did. Got switched if I forgot."

Betty sat next to Sam, who along with Sanford, filled the small plates on the coffee table with appetizers. "Did you two solve any problems while we were in the kitchen?"

Sam shrugged. "Sanford's thinking more about his future in the law profession."

Betty added snacks to her plate. "You have to tell Helen and me."

"I'm not sure how it will work." Sanford paused and looked at each in turn. "I want to practice law that helps people who haven't been as fortunate as I have, maybe even colored folks."

Betty set her plate down and sat up straighter. "Nice thought."

Sam grabbed her hand. "Betty, listen to him. I'm afraid what he has in mind won't earn him many friends or much business from either side."

Betty glanced at Helen who inclined a bit closer to Sanford.

"I'm going to represent anyone who needs a lawyer, not whites only. If a man of color needs a will made, or representation in court, I wouldn't turn him down."

Betty said, "We've got lawyers."

"Yes, but sometimes, a white lawyer generates more respect in a Louisiana courtroom in 1949." Sanford shook his head slowly. "Won't always be that way."

Betty grimaced and pulled back. "You've got a death grip on my hand, Sam."

"Sorry." Sam rubbed the marks on her hand. "Sanford and I learned a lot about equality fighting overseas."

Sanford said, "A man's a man, regardless of his skin color. I'd like to see all people treated more evenly here at home, and maybe I can help the colored people claim some of their legal rights."

"You won't be popular, might not have very many clients." Helen knifed off some cheeseball and slathered it on a cracker for Sanford. "But I believe you have the right idea. That's why I lobbied for the bookmobile. Not much, but it made a difference in our town of Jolson. My husband changed his viewpoint during the war, too."

Betty said, "You have to be practical. What if you don't get clients, of either race?"

"Then it's a good thing I have rich parents who love me." Sanford lifted a glass to his absent mom and dad. "Seriously, I know I'm fortunate, and because of that, I can do some things others couldn't."

"You mention your life plan to Burton?" Sam's words sounded casual, but Betty detected the edge in them.

"Ran the idea past Burton on our way home from your university. He wasn't in favor. He's got blinders on about the future. He's headed for his uncle's sugar cane farm. It's a big place and the uncle's kids aren't interested in running it. Burton never wanted a professional life. His folks will be glad he's settling. Burton's been doing too much drinking and gambling. Not a good combo."

An acrid smell filled the air, and Helen shrieked and raced to the kitchen. "Oh, no. I burned our main course. Oh, no. what will do?"

Sanford quickly wrapped her in his arms and brushed away her tears. "We'll eat noodles, the molded salad, the bread and a lot of dessert. We'll all put it on the table. The conversation is more important than the food, and the idea of us sharing a meal trumps conversation."

Betty enjoyed the ebb and flow of relaxed conversation around the dinner table. If she were blind, she wouldn't have known that the people sharing a meal had different colored skin.

With the dishes cleared, they began the evening's activity, composing an entry to claim the Merci Train wedding dress. They brainstormed ideas based on the missions of the Train of Gratitude of 1949 and the Friendship Train of 1947.

The Friendship Train collected food gifts from all Americans, rich, poor, all races, clubs, religions, school groups, and civic organizations. Everyone seemed eager to send food to those people suffering from shortages after the war. Then they talked about the Train of Gratitude, the Merci Train, sent by all the French citizens, wealthy, impoverished, children and adults. The two trains embodied the spirit of equality, generosity, and kindness.

They'd made notes, drafted and redrafted the essay and decided to submit the entry under the name, Miss B. Helen Jackson Warren. Sam and Sanford contributed their war experiences, which had been remarkably similar.

Betty fidgeted. "Our essay sounds good. What if we win?"

Helen draped an arm around Betty's shoulder. "If we win, I guess we'll both have to wear the dress. We are the same size."

Betty craned her neck up to see Helen. "Except that you're five inches taller than I am."

Helen refilled her pen and copied the final essay while the other three had another serving of cobbler with their coffee. Each reread the letter a final time before Helen licked a three-cent stamp and affixed it firmly on the upper right corner. She lifted her coffee cup. "Good luck to us."

All four stood and clinked coffee cups. "Good luck to us," they repeated.

With no warning, a rock crashed through the living room's bay window.

Tires squealed, and a motor revved in a hasty exit.

Helen's front lawn stood illuminated by the garish light of a fiery cross.

Chapter 14

Sam dashed toward the front door, but Sanford yelled for him to stop. "Wait. Let me check out front. You find the rock, see if there's a note. I'll get the hose."

"No water." Sam pointed to the blaze. "That's a gasoline fire. We'll need dirt or a tarp. I did learn a thing or two in my tank training."

Helen waved toward the back yard. "There's dirt mixed with potting soil in the wheelbarrow out back. Wanted to get my zinnias planted before…"

Sam and Sanford raced out the back, and Sanford carried a shovel while Sam pushed the barrow close to the fire.

Sam threw dirt on the cross with his bare hands, while giving sidelong glances at the homes near Helen's.

"Stubborn one." Sanford hacked at the cross with the shovel's edge, until the main part fell to the ground. He flung the remaining soil toward the flames that popped up in different locations like a jack-in-the box, surprising them with each new appearance.

"May I?" Sam took the spade from Sanford and slammed and hammered the charred wood, until he'd reduced the cross to a pile of hissing embers.

Sanford jerked him away from the blackened heap. "Come on, Sam. Let's put the wheelbarrow away."

"Show's over!" Sam shouted to the houses with closed doors and windows and kicked at the crackling, hissing residue. His anger at the situation burned as hot as the fire on Helen's front lawn. He'd kept his head down and his fists down his whole life. Why? He needed to get out of this place. Sam stalked inside and pounded on the dining room arched frame which rattled the light fixture.

"Are you okay?" Betty hurried to Sam's side and turned his shoulder, forcing him to face her. "You smell smoky."

"I am." Sam checked the door frame for sooty prints and started toward the kitchen. "I'll get a cloth and clean that off. Can't take my bad temper out on Helen's house."

In a couple of minutes, Sanford joined Sam at the kitchen sink. "I'm going to look on the bright side. I have an excuse to come back and see Helen. I'll sod that spot in her lawn and help her plant zinnias."

Sam accepted the towel and leaned against the counter. "We shouldn't have come here, Betty."

"Yes, you should." Helen's strident response quieted the room. "I've had three rocks through that window before."

"Why?" Sam waved to the overpowering stench in the front yard. "I think that was meant for Betty and me, telling us to get out of this neighborhood."

"Probably a cautionary notice for the four of us." Helen used a circling finger motion to include all. "People sent letters when I campaigned for the bookmobile on the other side of the tracks. And three messages arrived through the window tied to rocks, just like tonight."

Sam massaged the back of his neck. "I was so busy looking over my own shoulder, I never thought about what this evening might cost you and Sanford to invite us here. I'm sorry."

"I'm not sorry." Sanford looped the kitchen towel over the oven door handle. "I became better acquainted with a woman who acts on her beliefs, and that's someone I'd like to court. I'm even willing to be her guinea pig as she learns to cook."

"I can cook!" Helen placed hands on her hips.

Sanford tapped her shoulder. "I don't care if you can cook or not."

Sam thought Helen acted flirtatious when she replied to Sanford. "Well, I'd still like another chance. Why don't we all try this again after the bookmobile run on Thursday?"

Sam declined. "Not me. I'm going to stay out of trouble until I can finish my course work and leave for Nashville."

Betty demurred, too, but Sanford eagerly accepted. "I should check out the LSU Law School and scout out some housing close to campus."

Sam searched the other faces. Were they afraid? Anxious? The flaming symbol staked in the front yard hadn't frightened Sanford or Helen, but then their skin was white.

* * *

While Sanford waited in the car, Sam walked Betty to her front door where the porch light offered the only illumination.

"You still smell like smoke. Guess we all do." She twirled some hair around her finger. "Sam, I'm scared."

"Me, too." He grasped her hand, stopping its nervous movement. "Dean Keaton said I could finish early. But leaving...is that a coward's way out?"

Betty shook her head. "Maybe a brave man's way. You need to leave before something else happens."

"Sanford's waiting. I should go. Write me, please." Sam hugged her tightly, but only kissed her forehead. He already had too many wars waging inside his conscience to resurrect the marriage quandary.

As Sam scooted into the car, Sanford stretched his hand out the driver's window and over the roof to wave good-bye. "That Betty is one fine woman."

"You sound like my mother." Sam stretched his legs as far as he could in the front seat. "Thanks for going out of your way to take both of us to our homes."

"I didn't like what happened at Helen's." Sanford dimmed his headlights as he faced an oncoming car. "Guess I should expect more spineless criticism if I follow through on my lawyer plan."

"You might get your tires slashed, rocks thrown through a window, or offensive signs painted on your car or apartment, but I don't think anyone would hurt you or Helen physically." Sam mentally counted the white center stripes marking the paces toward his home.

Sanford remained silent, responding to Sam's hand signals, until he turned off the ignition in front of the Parker home. "So, Helen and I would be safe, but you and Betty might not be?"

"Sanford, you and I both grew up here. We know the facts." Sam placed his hand on the car door handle.

"Burton knifed me," Sanford said quietly. "I want you to know that I never believed his fabrication for a moment. In his mind, it was an accident."

Sam leaned against the door. "Then why did you ask me to explain what happened that day in the dean's office?"

Sanford drummed his fingers on the steering wheel. "Wanted to see what you'd say; you sidestepped giving an answer. He meant to kill you, for no other reason than the color of your skin, and because you were proud of your military service."

"You and I both survived." Sam opened the door and the dome light came on. "One lesson I've learned in my twenty-six years is that you don't look back. Oh, please tell your parents that I'm going to use the money they sent for medical school expenses."

"Good. Our world needs more doctors. But I'm not shocked. Dean Keaton already called. He says you're taking it in portions and that you plan to repay the fund. That makes it a loan, not a gift."

"And the Sanford Dickens Learning Fund will help train more than one doctor. What could be better than that?" Sam stepped outside the car, then ducked back.

"I'm glad we met, Sanford, and it's not because of the scholarship money."

"Me too. Serving on the Merci Train honor guard that day has changed at least four lives, five if we count Burton." Sanford moved the knob on the steering wheel back and forth. "We're getting much too serious."

"Right. Thanks again for the ride." Sam closed the car door and tapped the roof twice.

He watched until Sanford's taillights no longer glowed and considered what answer he should give Dean Keaton. The administrator stuck his neck out to secure permission for Sam to finish his course work early. He'd also figured out a way that Sam could accept the reward money and pursue medical school without holding extra jobs.

An early departure from Louisiana might make things safer for his family, for Helen and Sanford, and for his Betty. The four of them had spent the evening talking about the missions of the Friendship Train and the Merci Train, about a brighter future filled with equality and hope, but then came the cross.

Was the burning emblem the work of Helen's neighbor?

Was it Burton's farewell gesture?

Or could the mean act have been instigated by Claude Roark and directed at Betty? Or Helen? Or Helen and Betty?

Chapter 15

Hyacinths punched their fragrant heads out of the sweet earth as March roared out and April tiptoed in, bringing heady perfumed flowers and bees bouncing from one blossom to another. Betty had enjoyed her walk to the Gazette building, and today she snipped some yellow daffodils from her front yard to cheer up the mail room. After sorting letters, she placed the separate stacks in the basket and started the route which always ended with the editor.

"Mail, Mr. Roark. It's Betty Jackson. Do you have a story you want me to cover? Maybe something for Easter? How about a feature on Easter bonnets?"

"Come in and shut the door." The speaker wasn't old, bald, gruff Noah Roark. Today, Claude Roark sat in his father's swivel chair twirling a pencil through his fingers.

"Where's Mr. Roark?" Betty stood beside the door she'd left half open.

"My father and mother are on a long vacation, off to Niagara Falls. Mom wanted to go there on their honeymoon, but Dad had a paper to run, and they only made it to Houston. This month is their thirtieth anniversary, so they're going to New York City, then to the falls."

"Sounds like a good trip." Betty remained planted by the door.

"Dad turned the operation of the paper over to me. He'll continue as editor when he returns, but I'm now the managing director."

"Good luck," Betty said.

"Well, I guess my good luck is your bad luck, Betty. I'm making some cuts, and the mail delivery job is one we don't really need. Plenty of people running up and down stairs who can drop off letters, subscriptions, advertisements. Here's your final pay." He ripped a check out of the large ledger.

"Could I continue with news reporting?" Betty hated the piteous tone of her voice.

"No. That was something Dad did as a favor to me on behalf of Helen. That's over, which means your reporting career is also over. You don't need to come back."

The walk home took longer than her morning trip to the Jolson Gazette. A dark cloud blocked the sunshine, and a chill wind blew down the back collar of her blouse. Her mama always said "pride goeth before a fall," and Betty had been proud of her job in the newspaper building, even prouder when she wrote stories that appeared in the newspaper.

Now she needed another job. What? A choice of emptying bedpans at the hospital, changing sheets and doing laundry at a hotel, or cleaning houses loomed in the near future, perhaps for the rest of her life. Her dreams of holding an interesting, exciting job and looking polished and professional like Helen had been quashed.

* * *

A letter from Sam waited—something to enjoy over a reheated cup of coffee, the leftover in the percolator. Her back hurt, her legs cramped at inopportune times, and her arms ached. The definition of "bone-tired" revealed itself to her after she cleaned houses for only a few days. How had Mama done it for years on end? After only two weeks, she knew she didn't want to work as a cleaning lady the rest of her life. When the aroma of chicory wafted from the saucepan, she slit open Sam's envelope with a paring knife.

Sorry I haven't written more frequently. I study every night until I fall asleep, often with my head on a book instead of my pillow. I thought I could do all this before Easter, which as you know is the 17th. I've scheduled my final exams for Tuesday through Thursday. I've managed to cover all the material, but mastering it? I'm not sure.

Betty pressed his letter to her chest. She often fell asleep with her head on the table instead of a book. She hadn't told him about Claude Roark firing her, or her new job, or how exhausted she felt. Could she possibly find a job or jobs she could do while going to college? Sam had done it. Why couldn't she? She picked up where she left off.

Sanford moved from New Orleans to Baton Rouge because he received a spot in the fall law school class. Helen is decorating the apartment he rented. Sanford

96

calls me every other week to encourage me in my studies and tell me the progress of his plans. I'd love to pick up the phone and call you without worrying where the nickels and dimes would come from, but there would never be enough for me to talk to you as long as I want.

Betty's stomach rumbled and she sliced a piece of the spice cake left over from last night. She prolonged savoring the sweetness of the whole of Sam's letter, by even washing her plate, mug, and fork and putting them in the dish rack.

So, I'm asking if I can visit next Thursday night after I finish the last exam. I know that's a bookmobile night and the final stop is in your church lot. I'll bring sandwiches from Zach's for a picnic dinner, if that's okay with everyone. Would you mind if I headed toward Jolson as soon as I finish my last exam? Oh, Sanford invited me to sleep on his divan any time I visit.

Have a wonderful Easter celebration with your family. My little brothers and sisters are coloring eggs this week. It's a family tradition. We'll probably still do it when all the "kids" are fifty.

Have your stories made it to the front page yet? Save them for me. I want to read *every word you've written. I'll see you at the end of next week unless I hear from you.*

Your friend,
Sam

The bookmobile had been her only bright spot in the past two weeks. She and Helen now did runs on Tuesday and Thursday. The excitement about sharing a variety of books with eager readers seemed to comfort her aching back and sore muscles.

***

Betty saw Sam first, probably because she'd been checking the dirt road every few minutes. "Looks like dinner is here."

"And looks like you're too busy painting to eat." Sam eyed the wet paint on the bookmobile. "What happened?"

"Look at the other side." Helen finished the "E" in the all cap lettering of BOOKMOBILE on the near side.

Betty joined Sam on the other side. "Cruel, ugly words and pictures, but at least the people didn't destroy the bookmobile itself."

Sam held up the two paper bags. "Food or Paint?"

"Paint." Sanford waved a brush. "Let's finish the chores. We don't want undone work spoiling our dinner conversation."

The lure of sandwiches spurred quick completion, and after Helen spread a tablecloth from Sanford's car on the hard-packed dirt parking lot, Sam passed out sandwiches and sodas and then brought a metal opener from his pocket.

"You think of everything." Sanford pried the lid off his bottle. "If I'd been in charge, we'd be looking at the drinks instead of enjoying them."

When everyone finished, Helen stood. "I have an announcement. Miss B. Helen Jackson Warren is a finalist in the Merci Train Wedding Dress Contest. Our joint essay succeeded."

"That calls for dessert. Want to go to the Dairy Spot?" Sanford jingled his keys.

Helen waved the suggestion off. "We have to send in the waist measurement and a picture. I brought a cloth tape measure. Betty, you first."

Betty measured twenty-two inches. Helen measured twenty-four. They used Betty's Brownie to photograph Helen by the bookmobile, being careful not to touch the wet paint. Then they photographed Betty there, too.

Betty said, "I'm not the right height or the right color. Send in your picture Helen. Writing the letter together was fun, putting down a combination of Sanford and Sam's experiences, but we all knew I'd never wear that gown. Don't know if I'd want to. The gown is so gorgeous, I'd be afraid to put it on."

Sam put his arm around Betty's shoulder and rocked her side to side. "And the contest stipulated someone tall. You're no bigger than a minute."

"If our entry wins, Helen can put it on for photographs and then we can—well Helen and our mothers—can shorten it." Sanford looked for approval.

Sam shrugged. "Or we could leave it and Betty could stand on a box during the ceremony."

"But then she wouldn't get to walk down the aisle," Helen pointed out the problem with the box suggestion.

"And *she* would need a groom waiting at the altar," Betty said.

Helen snapped her fingers. "Betty, Betty. Can you guess who is going to tie the knot? No, of course you can't. Let me tell you. It's Claude Roark. He's marrying the lady who does the newspaper's social reporting!"

"The old spinster?"

"She's only two years older than I am. Yes, they'll be married and off on their honeymoon as soon as his mother and father get back from their thirtieth anniversary trip. Can you believe it?"

"Are you disappointed?" Betty watched Helen's face.

"No! I'm relieved. And I'm happy for both of them."

Sanford looked at Sam. "Any clue as to what's going on?"

Sam chuckled. "Nope. In fact I rarely know what's going on when it comes to the ladies."

Chapter 16

Sam placed the dean's Green Book, the list of restaurants and rooms for rent that accepted people of color, in the glove box. "Glad you're going along, Daddy. Even though I'm grown, it's comforting to have someone with me when I talk to the folks at Meharry and find a place to live in a new city." Sam jingled the keys. "Who's driving the first leg?"

"I'll ride." Lincoln Parker took the picnic basket from his wife of thirty years and patted his children's heads. "You mind your mama while we're gone."

The first hour passed in companionable silence, then Sam broached the topic he'd been considering for some time. "Daddy, how long did you and Mama know each other before you married?"

"You know that story." His father rolled down the window and rested his arm on the frame. "What do you really want to know? I may be old, but I still know when you have something on your mind."

"Betty." Sam let the name hang in the air. "I'm thinking maybe she could study at the university, too. We could scout around for a job she might like while attending classes. We could look for an apartment."

"One apartment or two?"

Sam sensed his father's gaze. "I don't know, Sir. Not sure I'm ready to tie the knot."

"You need to be sure. A lifetime's a long time, and that's what you promise when you put a ring on a gal's finger."

"Were you nervous about getting married?" Sam glanced from the flat section of the highway to his father.

"Sure. If any married person says different, they're probably lying."

"I'm also a bit uneasy about going on my own to a new city, a new school by myself. Went from home into the Army, then back home to go to Southern University. I've never lived on my own. Maybe I need moral support."

"If she's a crutch for your support, asking her to uproot her life would be unfair. If you want her to share this new beginning, that's something different. But I can tell you one thing, that old saying that two can live as cheaply as one is not true. If she goes to the university while you're going to medical school, you'll be eating a lot of beans and biscuits, even with your fancy scholarship."

"She's a real good cook. I bet she could even make beans and biscuits taste like a feast." Sam licked his lips, remembering the apple cobbler.

His dad leaned against the passenger door and faced Sam. "Another thing to consider before you bind yourself to someone for life is if you like that person. Betty's pretty as the dawn of a new day, but looks change. Do you like her? The time will come when 'like' is as important as 'love.' You don't make a life decision lightly. I'm going to get a little shut-eye before my turn to drive."

Sam checked the gas gauge, good for another eighty miles. Did he like Betty?

He did. He liked her zest for life, her courage, her determination to seek a reporter's job. He liked her love of family. He liked her family, and she liked his. If she hadn't fit in with the Parker clan, that would have been a red flag. He liked the caring part of her personality, the way she lavished love on those kids at the bookmobile. He liked the confidence she showed in maintaining a friendship with Helen. That was a two-way street, but it took gumption on Betty's part to reciprocate.

He did like her. He also cared about her hurts and disappointments. And heaven knows, he'd been physically attracted to her since the first time he'd seen her.

* * *

The first morning after they returned from Nashville, Sam sat on Mr. Jackson's front porch. He'd arrived before sunrise as Betty's father had suggested that might be the only time they could talk privately.

Sam whipped out a wedding ring set from his pocket and held it close to Mr. Jackson's face. "This is a family ring. My aunt and uncle never had kids, and they passed it on to me. They were married forty-two years before she died."

"Good omen, nice ring." Mr. Jackson replied solemnly, but Sam detected a twinkle in his eye.

"It is." Sam replaced the ring in his pocket. "I hope to be married at least that long."

"Admirable goal." Now the laughter in Mr. Jackson's eyes traveled to his lips which turned up in pleasure.

Sam rushed through his request. "Mr. Jackson, I'd like to have permission to ask Betty to marry me, and soon."

Mr. Jackson's face took on a stormy cast. "What are you saying?"

"I'd like to marry her so we can go to Nashville together. I'd never be able to concentrate on my studies without her by my side. She can go to college, too. I brought the paperwork, and my dad and I checked on some inexpensive apartments close to campus. I really want to marry your daughter by late May or early June." Sam rifled through the bag of papers he'd brought.

"So you want to marry my daughter?" Mr. Jackson leaned back and blew out a big breath.

Had the man thought Betty was in the family way?

"Yes, Sir. Of course. I do want to marry her, Sir." Sam spewed his words out in a jumble.

Mr. Jackson rewarded Sam's sputterings with a grin. "I think you already have Betty's heart, so you can have her hand, too. But a ceremony in a month? You know how womenfolk love to fuss over weddings."

Sam pumped Mr. Jackson's hand until Betty's father placed his other hand on top, stopping the vigorous motion.

"She'll be in charge of the bookmobile this evening. Helen Warren slips her a little extra money for helping. I better get ready for work." Mr. Jackson grinned. "Getting my permission is one thing, but Betty has a mind of her own.

* * *

After Sam's shift at Zach's Po'boys, Sam tucked the paper bag filled with information about Nashville, the college courses, and the apartments under his arm and set out for the bookmobile. He heard the words of his own father and Betty's father in his head.

A lifetime's a long time.

You already have Betty's heart.

Was he ready to get married? He'd shown her father the ring, asked his permission.

Maybe he should postpone asking her. It would be better not to ask than regret the decision later. He fingered the wedding band set in his pocket.

Was he looking to her to support his insecurity? Did he want a wife or just a confidante?

Then he saw her, sitting in a ring of children, reading and showing them the illustrations on each page. How could he have ever doubted? He needed her with him for a lifetime, and even that might not be long enough. And his heart belonged to the striking woman surrounded by little ones enthralled with her every word. He squatted behind the children and was soon ensnared in the tale of Pinocchio's transformation into a real boy—by the power of love.

After the children left and the bookmobile was locked, Sam knelt and held up the ring. "Betty, like Pinocchio needed Geppetto, I need your love to make sense of my life. Would you please marry me? And soon? I love you. I want us to start our new life in Nashville together."

Betty gasped and put both hands over her mouth and began to cry.

Had he misjudged? He got up and wrapped her in his arms. "If it's too sudden, we can wait. But if you feel the same as I do..."

Betty stopped his words by placing her lips on his.

Chapter 17

Betty sighed, then lifted her face to his for another sweet kiss. "You said 'soon.' When are you leaving?"

"Late May." Sam cupped her left cheek in his hand. "We could both get used to the campus. Maybe we could take a couple of classes during the summer, see how difficult they'd be. You could study journalism or learn to be a teacher. You're so good with children."

Betty placed her hands on his chest. "I can't think about college classes until we get married."

"That only takes about twenty minutes, right?" Sam shrugged.

Betty grasped him around the waist and placed her head over the spot where his heart raced. "The ceremony may be twenty minutes, but preparing for the exchange of vows takes a little longer."

"What should I do? Now that I'm sure I want to marry you, I want it to be as soon as possible. Oh Betty, I can't believe you love me." Sam traced the outline of her lips with his finger.

"I have to tell my parents." Betty grabbed his hand.

"They know. I asked your father. I did things right, very proper." Sam kissed her hand. "Want to tell Helen? She brought us together. Think she's still at the library?"

107

Betty checked her watch. "For another hour. Let's go. I need to tell someone the news or I'll burst."

"And you should wear the engagement ring if it fits." He slipped it on Betty's third finger, left hand. It fit perfectly.

She and Sam swung their joined hands on the walk to the library, and the motion made Betty feel like a carefree kid.

Sanford answered their knock. "Hello, you two. I'm pestering the pretty librarian until she closes. Come on in."

"We're not allowed inside, Sanford, but we do have news to share with Helen. We'll wait in the park." Sam indicated the stone seat facing the ring of flowers across the street.

Before they reached the bench, Helen barreled out of the library. "I hear you have something to tell me."

Betty held up her left hand, and Helen squeezed Betty so tightly that she had trouble breathing.

Helen released her fierce hug and focused on the ring. "Have you set the date?"

"Sam wants to marry in late May or early June. We're moving to Nashville after we're married." Betty adjusted the ring on her finger.

"How exciting for you both to start a new life in a new city. I'm so happy for you." Helen turned to Sanford. "Isn't this wonderful news, Sanford?"

"Wonderful." Sanford edged his way next to Sam, placing an arm on Sam's shoulder. He spoke to Sam in a voice meant for all to hear. "Sam, I need to ask you

108

something. Would you consider being my best man? You saved my life and introduced me to my true love, so you're my first choice."

Betty screeched. "Really?"

Helen nodded. "Really. And we have more news. Our joint essay is the winner of the Merci Train wedding dress contest. The committee selected our entry out of the three finalists. We won! We used my mailing address, so when we got the letter, Sanford and I went to New Orleans. I tried it on, and they photographed me and the other two ladies from every angle. The committee agreed it fit me best. And just like Cinderella's slipper, they awarded the fairy-tale gown to us."

"Helen had to sign papers accepting the gift before they would let her take it home. And they requested notification of our wedding day." Sanford beamed. "Helen said they would be invited for pictures prior to the service, but that our wedding would be a private family affair."

Helen clasped both of Betty's hands. "Isn't it exciting? Betty, you're going to look gorgeous in a wedding gown fashioned in France. I have the dress at home. Let's all go to my place. I'll have my assistant close the library today."

* * *

The ivory brocade gown stretched over the bed, the train cascading on the floor.

"Try it on, Betty." Helen ran her fingers over the rich material.

109

"Oh Helen, you know that Sam and I would both be tarred and feathered if I wore the dress. I'm just happy you'll get to wear it. And you know that Sam can't be Sanford's best man, and that I can't watch you march down the aisle." Betty heard the regret in her voice. Had the others heard it too?

Betty touched the luxurious texture of the fabric and wished for one brief minute that she actually could wear that special dress on her wedding day. But instead of a French couture dress, her garb would be homemade, but with every stitch sewn with love.

"Betty, would you consider wearing a second-hand wedding dress?" Helen's lilting tones hinted at a secret.

Sanford winked at his fiancée. "We've come up with a plan. See what you think. Helen and I could have a morning wedding. She could wear the dress first. Betty, you and Sam could marry in the afternoon with Betty wearing the dress. We can sign as witnesses for each other."

Betty and Sam both shook their heads no.

"You know we can't attend your wedding," Betty said.

"Hear us out." Helen intertwined her fingers through Sanford's. "I told Sanford that since I'm a widow, it wouldn't be appropriate for me to have a big wedding, and he and his parents came up with a spectacular idea."

Sanford nodded. "My father's a judge, so he can officiate, and my mother wants to have the ceremony in our garden. And don't worry about rain. If that happens, we'll move the whole thing inside. My mother makes better plans than any general. She'll be prepared for anything and everything."

Sam continued to shake his head. "Our families would never forgive us if we got married without them being there."

"Bring them all." Sanford threw his hands up. "I told my father I wanted you for my best man. My parents can't wait to meet you and your family. See where this is going?"

Betty tried to keep the excitement out of her voice. "But what about your other guests? The press? The people are going to want to see the bridal gown from the Merci Train."

"We'll have the photographers in first. My father, Judge Dickens, already stated there will be no press for the ceremony. Pictures only, and they are to be taken before the exchange of vows. My father offered to supply a story to go with the photograph." Sanford's excitement bubbled over, catching them all in his delight.

Helen took over where her fiancée's narrative left off. "Betty, you'll write the story of our wedding, won't you? I know you didn't want to be a social reporter, but make an exception for us." Helen stared at Betty until she nodded.

"We could write the story together. Then you can make sure I don't forget any detail," Betty said.

Helen wagged her finger. "Can't. Your mother, Sam's mother, Mrs. Dickens, and I are going to be very busy altering the gown for your afternoon wedding. I'm thinking we'll just hem the front of the gown. We want that long train to trail behind you."

"I'd never heard of the Merci Train, but two of its unique gifts have changed all our lives." Betty ran her fingers lightly over the long line of the skirt.

"Try it on," Sanford urged. "I can't imagine a better expression of the Merci Train's purpose than to have two brides sharing this exquisite frock."

Betty picked up the couture dress, marveling at its weight. "More important than sharing the gown is sharing a relationship with you and Sanford. The Friendship Train was sent with food for starving Europeans, and France sent these cars back to say thank-you."

"I'd say the goodwill of our two nations blossomed right here in Louisiana when the four of us became friends." Sam scooted closer to Betty. "You're going to look fantastic in that dress, Sweetheart."

"Join me in the kitchen." Helen led the way. "I have a bottle of champagne I've been saving for an extraordinary occasion, and I can't think of anything better than to toast our futures and the Merci Train which brought us all together.

The End

Afterword

In February, 1949, the freighter Magellan wearing a banner of *Merci America* arrived in   New York harbor carrying the Train of Gratitude laden with gifts from France and its citizens. Packaged in forty-nine boxcars, a car for each of the forty-eight states and the additional one for the District of Columbia and Hawaii to share, the presents represented the appreciation for the food sent to France in 1947 via the Friendship Train.

Each state received different items, from large pieces of furniture to small items of jewelry. A handful of states received wedding gowns. One of those held a Cinderella style contest for the winner, another state selected the recipient by virtue of an essay contest. The Louisiana dress actually went to a young lady who honeymooned in France and took the gown with her as a gesture of good will.

For information about the Merci Train and to find the location of the Merci Car in your state, please visit the website: http://www.mercitrain.org/.

THE MERCI TRAIN WEDDING DRESS

The humanitarian effort to feed people in need on the other side of the Atlantic Ocean, named the Friendship Train, was spearheaded by Drew Pearson, a Washington columnist, and every state plus Hawaii and D.C. participated. Historian Dorothy Scheele's website, www.thefriendshiptrain1947.org offers detailed information about the Friendship Train and the contributions of each state.

The characters in this book are from my imagination, and not based on any actual persons or events. The arrival of the Merci Train in Louisiana served only as a springboard for the creation of this fiction.

* * *

If you enjoyed this book, help spread the word by posting a review.

ABOUT THE AUTHOR

Linda Baten Johnson grew up in White Deer, Texas, where she won blue ribbons for storytelling. She still loves telling tales. She loves researching for her books and creating characters who have spirit and gumption.

Other books by Linda Baten Johnson:

The Friendship Train
Mystery of Desolation Point
Henry Goes to Texas (Young Texans Series)
Elsie and the Hurricane (Young Texans Series)
Tiny's Emancipation (Young Texans Series)
Kathleen's Vision (Orphan Train Riders)
Homer the Racehorse (with Katherine Loughmiller)
Her Christmas Cowboy
Orphan Train Bride-Healing Scars
Harvey House Girl-Recipe for Love
Searching for Joy
Forget Me Not
Magnolia Morning
Cocoa and Christmas Crackers
It Adds Up to Love
The Matchmaking Widow
Rich in Love
The Missing Groom

Connect with Linda at: www.lindabatenjohnson.com or email her at lindabatenjohnson123@gmail.com